Star-Hoppers...

MUNSFORD was Earth's emissary to the great Galactic civilization—his mission, to persuade them to conquer us.

LaRUE had invented a process that could save the world from starvation—if the world wanted to be saved.

HALSEY was a stock clerk. He translated ancient Scythian script at night, with hair-raising consequences.

WALTERS owned a process that could make him master of the universe—if he could get rid of the man who had mastered him.

Meet them all—and scores of other unforgettable characters—in the nine stories in this fifth collection of Star Science Fiction originals.

This is an original publication—not a reprint.

STAR
SCIENCE FICTION
STORIES
NO. 5

edited by

Frederik Pohl

BALLANTINE BOOKS • NEW YORK
An Intext Publisher

© 1959, by Ballantine Books, Inc.

Library of Congress Catalog Card Number: 53-5671

All rights reserved.

SBN: 345-02721-3-095

First Printing: May, 1959
Second Printing: November, 1972

Cover art by John Berkey

Printed in the United States of America

BALLANTINE BOOKS, INC.
101 Fifth Avenue, New York, N.Y. 10003
An Intext Publisher

CONTENTS

TROUBLE WITH TREATIES

by KATHERINE MACLEAN *and* TOM CONDIT

Katherine MacLean is a young lady of charm and talent—not the only one such among science-fiction writers, but nearly the only one who turns her back on the feminine-writing hallmarks (love— the family—children) in order to compete with the hairiest-chested males on their own territory. How well she succeeds, this story (her first in collaboration with Tom Condit) amply demonstrates.

Third Officer Llyllw, officer on watch of the scoutship *Wllyll'n* stared at the small object on the screen with a faintly puzzled expression on his furry face. The shape of the object failed to match any of the spaceships in his handbook, and yet it was undeniably a ship.

He reached for a phone circuit to call his superior officer, and then stopped without completing the move. Usually his thoughts were slow, but his conclusions were generally extremely accurate, and, as the commendation he had received last year put it, "most orderly".

Unidentified ship! All ships within the Empire of Erdig the Omnipotent were built to standard types. This ship could not be from any conquered part of the Empire. This meant an unconquered alien species, another world to be Brought to Order. It was an historic moment. Quietly, hoping that his superior officer would not appear behind him, he put tracers and radar amplifiers on the alien ship, and recorded the event in the bridge log, adding his name and the time with careful precision. It would pay to have his name connected with the discovery. It would make a good counterbalance to a reprimand, and he could see a reprimand coming up.

He turned again to the screen for a quick glance. The ship, now enlarged to seem larger and clearer, was very alien in design. He visualized alien beings inside, innocently pursuing their course, unaware that their chaotic lives were doomed to be Brought to Order. He remembered the delightful humbleness and obedience of slaves who had fueled their ship at the Thirty-Second World Brought to Order. It made a man feel good, having slaves around. The realization of the sacred Nll'ni mission to Bring Order out of Chaos spread a warm glow through him.

Journeyman Telepath Martin Jukovsky, of the exploration ship *Kemal Ataturk*, five months out of Pluto and bound ingalaxy, suddenly sat up and dropped his magazine. The green parrot on his shoulder lost its balance and flew away in squawking indignation.

"Hawwrrk! Angular Trisection! Awwrrk! Help! Help!"

"Shush up," said Jukovsky absently, searching for the trail of strange thoughts he had crossed so briefly. Something about Order out of Chaos . . . Had someone on the ship gone mad? The thought had a very strange feeling about power over *people,* and a mixture of terror and triumph . . . He found the flavor again, and thought rapidly along the fading trail of faint thought, trying to think and feel like that, tuning in, establishing an empathy. Suddenly he was tuned in, the other's personality swirling into his mind in a hammerblow of frightened emotions and cold calculating thoughts.

[*Slaves* (pleasure) . . . *Alien Ship on screen* . . . *Reprimand?* (fear) *Promotion* (fear) . . . *War* . . . *Bring to Order* . . . What on Earth did that mean? Where was— *Alien Ship* . . . (emotions)]

"Holy Dancing Dervish!" Jukovsky gasped, and ran barefooted to the control room to push the emergency alarm button.

Bells jangled throughout the *Ataturk*. The helmsman leaped to his feet. "Hey, that's the emergency alarm," he shouted over the din. *"Hey, Jukovsky, what's the idea?"*

"Spaceship!" Jukovsky made a preoccupied gesture

and lowered himself into a chair and started on the difficult task of tuning the other telepaths on board to the thoughts he was tracing. They came in—first Tewazi, Zorn and Candleman in a blast of curiosity, and then Hahn, disengaging himself from some far-off thought to slide in with the rest. He knew each of them, could feel as he came in: Tewazi, coolly analytical, organizing information; Zorn inquisitively searching and tracing; Candleman eagerly grasping; Hahn watching, emotions—so quiet he seemed completely unemotional—permeating his thought. They gripped and followed the thought trail.

On board the *Wllyll'n*, Third Officer Llyllw was beginning to feel his fur prickle with an eerie sensation of being watched. He looked hastily over his shoulder and saw nobody. He reached for the general-alarm cord. It should have been pulled the instant the alien ship was identified as alien, but he could be executed for pulling it without orders. It was time to call the Second Officer, or even the Captain. He could be questioned about the delay. Llyllw gripped his courage and went a step closer to insubordination. With a steady hand he flipped the switch that awoke the ship's main computer.

The computer, Infallible Regulations and Advice, was usually used for navigation and landings, but it was also the ship's authority for military regulations, precedents, and all rulings of his Exalted Omnipotence Erdig, Supreme Ruler of Nll'ni and Lord of Creation. The Infallible could check and recognize screen images of all known ships, and should be able to cope with an unknown ship. There were after all a number of regulations and precedents dealing with the Bringing to Order of an alien species.

He waited. The ship's screens blinked as the big computer cut into them and started watching. He waited another instant, wondering if the computer would react. His life hung in balance.

The alarm buzzers went off with a deafening roar. The computer had recognized the emergency. A recorded voice began barking orders over the speaker system. He was safe.

Llyllw took a deep breath and held it while he calculated. Now the Second Officer, the First Officer, the Captain, and the Strategic Captain had been by-passed.

They were all going to be angry and out for his blood. He balanced this out against the fact that the Infallible Code would have his actions in its record. If he could keep himself from being executed on some pretext, until the ship returned to base, the High Servants of the Exalted Omnipotence would be well pleased with him,— they liked to have senior officers aware that the Infallible could be consulted and recordings made without their consent—it helped them fear Erdig as they should. A promotion to a different ship . . .

The computer voice was roaring over the speaker system:

"Full Military Alert. Full Military Alert. Strange Ship sighted. Hold Fire, Await Orders. Repeat Hold Fire, Await Orders. All listed experts, linguists, and personnel with contact experience un-Nll'nian species stand by for direction if off duty. Full Emergency. Repeat. Full Emergency. Ship Command ordered to turn over absolute authority to Strategic Captain. All personnel consult written regulations RMZZ947 on Bringing To Order of Alien Species."

The First Officer was first onto the bridge, although he had not been closest. He bounded up the ladder from his quarters, roaring, his eyes blurred and his fur matted. Obviously he had been sleeping during a Self-Improvement period.

"Who turned information over to the Infallible?" he snarled glaring around wildly. "You, you're the watch officer! What the idiocy is the idea?"

Lllyllw concealed the Nll'ni version of a smile and grovelled politely against a bulkhead, hiding his head.

"My abject apologies, Your Authority. The object was sighted at such a distance that there was no certainty that it was truly a ship. I did not want to disturb my Excellent Superiors for a matter which might be only a criminal error of judgment on my part, so I turned the problem over to the Infallible, to be sure of correct action, if only in my own deserved execution for mistaking a natural object for a ship."

There was a pause while the First considered the case. The regulations allowed the lowest crew member to consult the Infallible any time it was not busy with another problem. It was an insult to one's superiors to take any such action without orders, but technically it was not a personal move, merely a consulting of regulations.

"Face out!" The First had his expression under control and his fur sleeked when Llyllw turned. "Very good, a most patriotic action," the First Officer complimented him stiffly. "Quite correct—by the regulations."

Third Officer Lllyllw stiffened and saluted with precision. Behind the expressionless masks each could see the hatred and ambition in the other's eyes. It is a long hard climb to become Captain of a ship, and your fellow officers are very much in your way.

Several thousand miles away, in the other ship, Master Telepath Tewazi muttered half-hysterically as he leafed through the *Handbook of Comparative Sociology*. "Diu! There must be something like this in here somewhere!"

The four young Journeyman Telepaths were recording full speed on stenotypers, wincing occasionally at the thoughts they were recording. . . .

There was a hush on the bridge of the *Wllyll'n* and everyone grovelled against the bulkheads as Strategic Captain Bryllw hoisted himself up through the hatchway. He was fat and greying, and wore a captain's uniform in purple, indicating a retired captain. He was seldom seen by the others on the ship, passing his time viewing history tapes and playing games of logic with the computer, in private. Retired Captains of much experience and success were the only ones permitted to have the berth of Strategic Captain on a military ship. It was a pleasant way for an old military man to retire, for usually there was nothing to do, except view tapes and work at hobbies.

"Who sighted the ship?" he growled.

Llyllw raised a hand, keeping his face to the bulkhead.

"Uh! Get around, all of you, There's more to do than cling to the wall like a flock of Moragais!"

The officers and hands on the bridge stood at trembling attention as Bryllw looked them up and down. They had heard of his reputation as a martinet from the days he had commanded three ships.

"There is an emergency and I shall demand intelligence and skill from you. I know this is asking much, but you will start making an effort to apply your bean-sized brains to the problem of this alien ship."

The Captain's and Officers' hackles rose at the insult, but their expressions did not change and they stared rigidly ahead.

"*You!*" The grizzled Strategic Captain leveled a finger at the Navigation Officer, who was standing trembling in the rank behind the Captain. "Are all star maps prepared to be destroyed or scrambled on four-seconds' notice?"

The unfortunate Navigation Officer swallowed and cleared his throat. "No, Excellency."

"They should be," Bryllw let a silent moment pass while he watched the Navigator inquiringly.

The officer, expecting immediate execution, realized slowly that Bryllw was waiting for something. "Your pardon, Excellency. May I be dismissed so that I may make preparation to destroy or scramble all star charts?"

"A most sensible plan," Bryllw purred. "Dismissed."

He waited until the unfortunate Navigator was down the ladder. Then he addressed the rigid group. "Believe it or not, oh, Assembly of Wisdom, there is a remote possibility that we might have met a species capable of destroying us, and they might want to know where our home planets are."

He directed his glower at the Captain, standing at attention with the others. "Inferior, our ship is now overtaking the alien ship. What do we do when we come within range?"

"Open fire," the Captain snapped, glaring at the wall.

"Brilliant, Your Wisdom. I hope you did not strain your brain irreparably." That was a snarl, only barely disguised as a smile. The smile vanished, and the grizzled Strategic Captain stood back a yard and let out a bellow that made them all jump.

"You miserable imbeciles! That ship contains the only opportunity you will ever have to locate and trace a new species, and add a new planet to the Empire of Erdig. If they have detected us, they might already have destroyed all maps. And you morons want to help them, by using their ship for target practice and blowing it to bits, so that we will never be able to assemble any information from the pieces."

He lowered his voice to a simple tone like an adult explaining to children. "We must talk to them, make sure that they are not afraid of us, you understand? We must—"

He turned abruptly to the Gunnery Officer. "Inferior, your long-range guns are already trained on the target, preparing to blow this valuable ship to bits. Am I correct?"

The Gunnery Officer seemed to have difficulty answering. "Gugh, ah Yess, Authority. Military alert . . ."

"I am glad to see you are so efficient." Bryllw purred. "Are the crews instructed to fire automatically if the defense screens register unusual radiation?"

"Not without further orders, Authority."

"Wonderful! Then this valuable source of information will not be blasted out of space, while I am trying to explain how to seem friendly. It is safe even if they signal us on an unusual wavelength. Wonderful. It must be an accident."

He smiled, a genuine expression, and the trembling group of officers dared to take a few deep breaths and consider themselves out of danger. "We must go softly in approaching these creatures. We cannot be a warship, we must approach them as civilians, like a trader ship. Please study to act like civilians. Anyone who has associated with civilians or bought from traders in civilian stores please show the others how civilians act. We will be learning their language, humbly so as to trade with them, you understand, and whoever is in front of the viewscreen must seem like a civilian, and very humble and polite. You understand?" He looked at their rigid faces and detected signs of resistance, and stood back to bellow again.

"Let us have no show of pride, no signs of Nll'nian superiority. Is that clear? Anyone who gives the slightest indication that this is a warship, or that he personally is accustomed to weapons of war, will be executed—immediately!"

The grizzled warrior looked at the rigid and trembling officers and men with satisfaction. He lowered his bellow to a conversational tone.

"I am going to retire to my quarters and leave the opening moves to you, Captain. Remember that these creatures do not know anything about us, and present to them whatever lie is least alarming. Do not consult the Infallible or make any change of plans without first consulting me."

He smiled at the rigid group. "To save us from the pain and embarrassment of many executions, I will remove the need of your committing errors by conducting the preliminary negotiations myself. Call me as soon as you have managed a rough translation of the alien's language and have the translation machine working."

He descended the ladder clumsily, but he did not look at all ridiculous.

Captain Rablyn moved from his position of frozen attention, and looked after the Strategic Captain with a snarl.

Aboard the *Ataturk* Master Telepath Tewazi called a conference. He leaned back and shut his eyes as the telepaths about the ship answered the call and tuned in with their reactions.

["Hooboy, do they like each other!"

"Like a nest of rattlesnakes."

"He's a tough old bird, that Bryllw."

"Let's get this coordinated a little. Somebody start verbally repeating for Chang. This is his type of situation: he ought to be coordinator." "Too bad he's not a telepath ...

"What a nutty culture." ... I'll do it." "We must convince

"Like a fruitcake, like our ancestors." Bryllw that we are friendly, so he will

"What?"

leave us alone."

"Leave us alone? You weren't tuned in to "Yes, Look up those nuts. No use trying to get them Authoritarian in the to change their minds." handbook. They never change."

"But Gandhi ..." "Not correct," (Hahn) "Psy-

"He'd like that. Bryllw would like chological reorientation. no resistance ... encourage him, to Takes time, though." attack."

"Strange attitude." "Time! ... (obscenity) ..."

"Get that Order-Chaos bit? Look up "We don't have time Efficiency Expert. *They* never change. change him. Outsmart him."

"His officers dislike him,   "How?" "Find out from him,
Crew very favorable though . . .   what would make him
Maybe something there . . . like the   leave us alone."
Bounty, only different."   "I couldn't follow him at all."
"What *Bounty* . . ." "(image, impressions)"   "Strange at-
"Oh." titudes, yes."   "He'll accept us at a certain re-
"He's worried that lationship. "Can we negotiate? What
we might be   is this relationship—I don't get it—(con-
more powerful. If he thinks so   cept of slave)" "Get off my
he'll be back off his ship and run."   lap, cat." *"This* ship,
"Chang says we can scare off   outpower the *Wllyll'n?"*
Bryllw." "Dammit, cat!" "With what? His ship is a killer,
"What's a   and it's fast. We can't beat them." "Chang's
slave?"   talking." "Chang says, run bluff, like poker."
"Huh?" "Ouch!"   "What's poker?" "What's a slave?"
"Why ouch?"

"Non-telepathic card game, depends on   "Cat clawed
not knowing what cards are in other's   me."
possession. Cards are strength.   "A slave is one who takes
Bet on outcome, pretend strong cards,   your orders. Must
frighten opponent so he   take them. "Why take orders if
will concede without struggle   you don't agree with them?"
to test you. That's bluff."   "Force. (image of) head coming
"But if he knows you might bluff?"   off.) That's why."
"Too much to lose if he   "Rights?" "No rights. Slave con-
tests and you're not bluffing.   sidered inferior species."
He doesn't dare chance it."   "Like a pet?" "No."
          "Repeat that for Chang!"
"But he told me."   "Inferior subservient species." "Like
          the cat?"
"What's so (vague obscenity) subservient about the cat?"
          "I've got an idea!"]

Some five hours after video contact had been established, Bryllw emerged from the schooling chamber with a rough knowledge of Terran, and the information that the ship he was facing was the patrolship *Vengeance* of the Terran Federation Frontier Guard, her captain was named Chang, and he was most grateful to the Nll'ni for taking on the task of linguistics involved in establishing contact.

Bryllw smiled a slow, murderous smile. Delightfully vivid in his memory were the pictures of all the idiotic actions the Terrans had performed in passing across key words: throwing balls in the air, smiling, frowning, gnashing their teeth, holding up one, two, three, four fingers. . . . These clowns should be a pushover.

He stepped to the video and looked into the face of the Terran framed in it. He began to speak, phrasing his thoughts carefully in the strange tongue. "I iss Bryllw, caftan ship here. Wooe desthire thrhade wiss you. Wooe seeging egtension Nll'ni thrhade rhoutes. Arr' you ooant thrhade? Much bhenefitus ourh people—yourhus aand minuh. Thrhade," he concluded, in a carefully memorized sentence "iss life blood of induthry."

Chang assumed his blandest expression, and his voice rolled out of the speaker unctuously. "As Frontier Guards we are, of course, entrusted with the safety and security of the peaceful citizens of our Federation. However, in view of the objective circumstances, and taking into account historical factors such as the Corn Laws, the assassination of Boris Stambouli and the relative success of the Wafd, it seems to us upon viewing the situation dialectically," the Nll'ni computer whirred, sending out whole lines of random symbols. "Viewing the situation dialectically, I say, it would seem that in the light of Thomas Jefferson's views on free trade it is incumbent upon us to place both shoulders on the ground, put our feet to the wheel, and consider the matter more intensively—with diligence, so to speak. If you would care to send a delegation on board our ship to further identify yourselves, we will be pleased to engage in discussion upon the matters previously alluded to. Otherwise," Li paused, "We shall be forced, much to our sorrow, to destroy you."

As soon as the screen went blank Bryllw turned to the officer in charge of linguistics. "Well," he roared, "what did he say?"

"There appears to be some difficulty in translation, Your Extreme Sentience, but it would appear that we are invited to send a delegation on board their ship to negotiate."

"Excellent!" Bryllw purred, and stalked off, leaving the linguist staring hopelessly at the tape in his hand.

By the time Bryllw's lifeboat reached the side of the *Vengeance/Ataturk,* bearing the Strategic Captain and five others, including Third Officer Llyllw, that officer had almost succeeded in banishing the feeling of being watched. As a matter of fact, he hadn't been watched for hours, since he was no longer important. It was Strategic Captain Bryllw who now struggled to conceal his uneasiness . . . He attributed it to the weird appearance of these skinny hairless things called Terrans. And, after all, this was his first experience of bringing a new species to order, though he doubted if any of the crew realized it. . . . A man could expect to be a little nervous about something like this, couldn't he? His mind wandered back to a campaign he had just missed when he was a Second Officer. . . . A race of primitive chlorine-breathers inhabiting the lone planet of a hot new sun. The planet was untenable to Nll'ni and its people incapable of accepting Order, so they had been exterminated to prevent any possibility that they might upset the Order of the Universe. The planet had been wiped clean of all life to prevent re-evolution and a small amount of mining activity had been commenced. It had been an arduous and expensive job, but it would have been highly disorderly to leave it undone.

Aboard the *Ataturk,* Tewazi reeled with dizziness and nausea, and dropped the *Handbook of Comparative Sociology*...

["Diu!"

"Uggh . . . Did you read Bryllw just then?"

"No, what . . . oh he . . . better tell Chang." "I will."

Quiet thought came in from Hahn: "Maybe we ought to blow up our ship at that. Tell Chang to make the arrangements or . . . Candleman, you in the engine room? Better rig something up just in case. Don't want these people to find Earth."

"An entire species, a whole planet . . ." "I don't think I want to read Bryllw any more."

Hahn again: "Stay clear, man . . . We have to out-think him."

"Chang says that if we suicide, we'll have to take them with us. We were making a pretty standard orbit out from the system when they saw us. All they have to do is check the records and trace our orbit back."

"Bryllw hasn't thought of that." "He will. And don't forget that computer."

"Stick by the plan.—]

Bryllw came into the Terran spaceship somewhat ruffled from the manhandling he had received in the airlock. He had been briskly and expressionlessly searched, and both his hidden weapons and his camera had been taken from him. The searchers had not been impolite, but neither had they been respectful: they had handled him like a piece of furniture.

"Humble," he muttered to himself in Nll'ni. "Be humble, trader." He surveyed the scene before him with widened eyes, trying to look like a recruit with his side-fangs not grown yet. The Terrans looked as bad as they had over the video, if not somewhat worse: obscenely smooth and hairless, their skins in various shades of light and dark brown. They looked scrawny and frail. It would probably be easy to force information out of one of them: he could be broken in the hands.

[Ugh!" "Diu!" (Hahn)—"Give me a *schlager* and I'll show that big ape who can be broken in the hands . . . second thought I can do it with my hands." "Cut it, man, you're as bad as he is." "You're too modern, Zern, don't understand combat."]

They wore almost no cloth to cover their hairlessness— a harness around the loins and some with a large green ornament on the shoulder. Of the six Terrans gathered to greet him, four had the green ornaments—the largest just a foot high . . . maybe the size indicated authority and could indicate which of the Terrans facing him were of importance.

While he stared at an ornament it moved, said a few words in Terran, spread large green wings and flew out of the room. Bryllw started. There had been nothing said about any green flying creatures while he was learning the language.

One of the Terrans stepped forward. "I am Chang, Co-ordinator today."

Bryllw paused to consider the strange title, then dismissed it and proceeded with his speech. "I iss Bryllw. You me talk viewscthreen. I iss vissneth manazherh andh arrithmetithian of thrhade ship *Wllyll'n*." He spoke briskly, convinced that he was speaking the language perfectly. "Ve thrhade. I tell rhulerh-serhvantth minh. Ve sendh ships worhldh yourh. Brhing many goodh thingth. You take. What you havh nont we havh. Ve havh nont you havh. Show me star map yourh planet. Wherh you people planet? Ve send merschant ship."

It was a good thing Chang did not have to understand him. Chang stepped forward trying to look formal. He took a long deep breath, rounded his voice, and began. "We of the Federation always welcome contact with new species. We hope for amicable relations, and hope that amicable relations can ultimately, or even immediately blossom into understanding and interdependence. In the record of history this historic meeting may be recorded as truly historic and might even mark the first step in a long history of friendship and friendly relations between our species and even of brotherhood and federation."

Bryllw's attention wandered. He had not fully understood all that was being said, but it sounded like the usual formal preliminaries.

"You forgif smaller self, Authority, what iss Federation."

"Ah—Federation is many planets mutually helping."

Chang resumed the speech, and Bryllw's attention wandered again. The claim to be many planets could be a standard bluff intended to scare him off, or it could be true. He noted with satisfaction that the interior of the ship looked primitive and unarmored, with few safety devices. If this ship were the best frontier guard the "federation" could put up, it would be better if they did hold a large number of planets. It would be easy to take them away from such a puny navy as this. The more planets the better.

["Awk! That's not the reaction we wanted!" "He knows about bluffs!" "We aren't scaring him off."]

Oblivious of trouble, Chang droned on . . .

". . . And, as I emphasized in our previous conversation, in the light of our reverence for the free trade views of such historical figures as Thomas Jefferson and Al Capone, it would seem inevitable that in the course of history we would be led . . ."

While the Terran orated on, the other five members of the Nll'ni boarding party came through the airlock one by one. They were breathing heavily and their weapons were missing, but they were still a good fighting force.

Bryllw wondered if the Terrans were afraid of them. If they were, it would indicate that the Terrans, unless they were arrant cowards, thought of themselves as relatively defenseless and weak.

He tried a feint. Abruptly he coughed in a loud rumble, and moved forward in a sudden jerk, then stopped himself with a hand apologetically against his faceplate as if to smother a cough, and stepped back again. It had worked, he had seen what he wanted to know. All the spindly two-legged creatures had flinched or frozen at his sudden motion and roar, and now, stiffened, were making a desperate effort to look nonchalant, and to resume their former attitude of interested listening to their leader's speech.

Unless they were cowards, that meant that they knew they were inferior to him. Bryllw decided that it might be possible to take the ship from these skinny Terrans with just bare hands and good discipline. Once they had the ship it would be easy to decipher the star charts and find out where its home planets were. However, if he continued on this act of being a meek trader, they might even tell him where the home planets were and save the need of fighting.

"Llyllw," he mumbled into the tiny intercom mike in his helmet. "Be prepared for action and keep a good watch for their weapons. They must have some, probably trained on us, but I have not seen them. I may try to seize this ship, as soon as I find out what these green flying things are."

["Get Taylor to work up some phony hand weapons in a hurry." "Why not use the ones we took off the gorillas?" "They'd recognize them, and know for sure we don't have any of our own. You don't want to wrestle with these characters." "What did we let them on the ship for?" "To frighten them, man."]

"Authority," Llyllw's voice came nervously over the intercom into Bryllw's helmet. "One of these green animals is speaking to me privately. I don't know what it is saying."

Bryllw looked back and saw Llyllw standing stiff and woodenfaced, with a green creature perched on his shoulder. The creature was staring at him, turning its head to stare with one eye at a time with an air of impolite incredulity.

"Awwwrk!" the creature suddenly screamed in commanding tones. "Tripledeck deal! Tripledeck deal!"

Llyllw went up into the air a foot, and came down even more wooden. The creature spread large green wings and flew off down the passageway. With a great rustle and whirr of wings the others took wing from the Terran's shoulders, and followed down the passageway until they were out of sight.

"You must excuse the Wraxtax," Chang said. "Their people have no custom of courtesy to strangers. You don't have to obey his command. We will explain to him."

"Who was he, Authority?" asked Bryllw, remembering to be humble. "Is he in command of any power in your great ship?" Who was in charge of this ship? The attitudes of each Terran to the other were ambiguous, neither indicating command nor obedience, and their attitude to the green winged things was even more peculiar and hard to identify. It made him nervous.

"He is not in command over anyone," Chang explained solemnly. "We are equals. The Wraxtax are the fifteenth species to join our Glorious Federation. I am not really an authority on them. Would you like to see the ship?"

Equals? Equals meant interchangable units, identical quantities. How could a Biped be an interchangable unit or an identical quantity to a Green Bird? And who was in charge? Bryllw knitted his brows staring earnestly at the Biped who had told him he was Captain. Was this nervous creature who was not saluted by his fellows really an Officer? He retracked through the statement and remembered the question. At least that was something clear, and he knew what he wanted.

"Ve must thrade science skillsh. Whant to see control room and enshine room, if pleassing to Your Authority."

The Terran showed his teeth and ducked his head in a gesture Bryllw had learned was friendly. "Very pleasing. Follow me."

Bryllw motioned his five Nll'nians in spacesuits to follow, wondering at the stupidity shown by non-Nll'nian species. They filed along a narrow corridor and through several hatches into a control room, where the Terran solemnly showed them the controls.

"The feeblevetzer is here, this switch and this meter. It is useful only in moments when one wants to exceed the speed of light and does not care in what direction one goes. The Bilateral Fort Allerton is here . . . this dial . . . and that lever . . ."

Bryllw stood confused, unable to follow the Terrans explanation. Terran was obviously a more complex language than they had thought. The dials and switches and screens of the control board looked precisely like dials and switches and screens with no hint of their use. Perhaps if he could see the machinery . . .

"Enshine room. See enshine room, Your Oberlord?"

Again there was no objection. As Bryllw followed, amazed at the stupidity of the Terrans, he spoke softly into his throat-mike to halt his men. "Don't all follow me. Four of you stay in the control room, stand around asking questions, look innocent, try to see where they keep any weapons and be ready to kill them and seize the ship when I give the order."

[Hahn: ". . . Ohhh . . . our friend is clever."]

"I don't see any weapons, Authority," Llyllw reported, his voice coming in tinnily on the earphone. "I'm last in line, and one of the Terrans is following us and pointing a framework of wires at us. It is about two hands square, and looks just like wires. The green things just flew in."

"Don't move suddenly, Idiot. Look peaceable and ask questions about their language and number system. Pretend you don't notice he's pointing anything at you. Keep someone wandering around behind him, and be ready to kill him when I give the word."

["!"]

"Hey Taylor," Hahn called cheerily in the control room. "Know Pig Latin? Utpay ouryay ackbay gainstagay ahay ulkheadbay, otgay itay?"

Bryllw was disturbed as he walked down the corridor. A framework contraption of wires a *weapon*? Where would you get the power? And why did the majority of the Terrans wear neither uniforms nor weapons? They wore only skin and harness, not suitable for hiding weapons, and with no insignia of rank. How could the ship be organized in any orderly fashion if there was no way to tell who was in command of what?

["What's bothering him now? We know who does what in the crew, why should anyone wear a label?" "It's Authoritarian custom to wear a label, makes them feel happier." "I read that part in the Handbook, but he seems to think it is *practical*! I mean. . . ." "Be clear, man . . . let's follow this."]

A ship could not run without some indication of rank and authority, Bryllw thought uneasily, and his skin prickled again with that strange, watched feeling. Perhaps the Terrans had taken off their uniforms and insignia to conceal some vital information about themselves. Perhaps they were not so helpless as they seemed, and were playing some game of considerable depth and darkness.

["Hoo . . . now he's starting to get a little nervous." "But why?" "The way we really are, he thinks it's a lie." "The way we really are is the Bluff?" "What?" "Now *you're* making *me* nervous."]

Bryllw moved carefully along another line of logic. The presence of the green flying creatures meant that the Terrans had expanded across at least two solar systems, for they would not find an identical atmosphere in their own solar system, and these "Wraxtax" showed no signs of wearing airsuits. By the laws of probability, it took exploring at least five systems to find a planet with identical atmosphere. It would appear that the Terrans had done a lot of exploring before encountering the Wraxtax. The spokesman had said that they were the fifteenth species to join the Terran "Federation". (What in space was a "Federation"?) The question was, which species dominated the other? One had to dominate, or you could never have any stable Order. The green creatures had done no work in his presence and had given only one order, which was ignored. It was all very confusing.

"Which one of the planets of your Fetheration is central one, Authority?"

"I don't understand," said Chang. "Suns are central, not planets. Of course it is conceivable that a system might exist . . ."

"I mean, vhich one carries out the government, isshues the laws?"

"Government? Laws?" Chang considered a moment, looking at the bulky spacesuited figure. "Oh, well . . ."

One of the other Terrans stepped forward hastily and spoke into his ear. Chang smiled.

"Why, it's a federation. All worlds are central."

"All worlds are central?" repeated Bryllw, trying to sound merely stupid. A red haze gathered in front of his eyes, and he lowered over the Terran with his hands dangling open. It was an effort to hold himself from picking the creature up like a doll and ripping its limbs off. He had climbed to the rank of captain half a lifetime ago so that he would not have to listen to insults from anyone except the High Servants of Erdig themselves. It was enraging to have a small hairless caricature of a creature, destined to be a slave, insolently telling him obvious lies, insulting his intelligence, and probably laughing at him.

"All worlds are central, you said, Your Wisdom?" He forced himself to be humble, though his voice was shaking. "But I like know vhich world has most power over the others."

"No world exerts power over any other world." repeated Chang blandly. "Why would any world do that? It would involve a most unprofitable expenditure of energy and resources and would probably lead to hostility. While we are stopped here, would you care to look at our atmosphere control division?" He stepped through a hatchway and out of reach.

Bryllw lumbered after him, bending his head in a determinedly humble pose. If he went amok now, his subordinates would claim he was senile. Perhaps they'd be right. He was shaking, but under control. Tewazi eased away from behind him.

[Woof! Did you feel that rage?" "It swamped me . . . I almost tried to strangle someone myself." "Me, too—Him." "No point telling Chang how close he came."]

Bryllw found himself in a small room, jampacked with equipment, tanks of liquid lining the walls. The strategic captain pretended to be studying the equipment while he got his thoughts under control.

As his breathing came back to normal and he stopped shaking, he focused on the tanks of liquid. They were glowing with intense illumination and giving forth reflected light to the rest of the darkened room. Each tank had a different form of vegetation growing in it, and each contained small golden creatures, swimming about and poking at the plants with their noses. At one side of each tank was a miniature bank of levers and dials, *inside the tank.*

Bryllw stared at the tiny control boards, then at the golden swimmers. Who would use the boards in there? The fish?

He cleared his throat, then remembered his Terran again. "What arrafp . . . what do these creatures, Authority?"

"Them I am an authority on. They are our atmosphere control experts, members of the twenty-fifth species to join our glorious federation."

"Forgive request, Authority, but . . . would inthroduce me? They such beautiful creatures . . ." Bryllw was thinking fast. The fish things were captives possibly, discontented slaves. Divide and rule . . .

Chang smiled blandly. "I'm afraid that they don't converse much."

Bryllw looked at the table. A pair of earphones lay on it, wires leading to one of the tanks. Obviously the Terrans conversed with the fish things. He hesitated.

The Terran moved to the door. "Shall we go to the Engine Room now?"

Bryllw followed him. The idea of negotiating with little golden fish was utter madness. Yet, logically . . . Logically, what?

(Who thought up that earphone rig?") ("I did.") ("Nice work, Jukovsky, he's reeling.") ("Hurry the guys up with the thinbumbob, that Strategic type is coming.")

As they walked down the corridor, a man dashed forward from the next hatchway and spoke hurriedly to Chang. The conversation looked unnatural, as all such actions of the Terrans had, and Bryllw realized it was because there was no form of salute exchanged and neither party went to attention while speaking. They were keeping their relative status a secret from him with fantastically good acting.

The Terran with him (the Captain?) turned from the brief conference and looked up at Bryllw, showing again those even white teeth that would be no use for anything except eating vegetables. There was something reassuring about the pacifism of his appearance. It calmed Bryllw's wild speculations about deadly conspiracies, though it failed to clear the fog which was gathering in his mind.

"I receive word," said the Terran, "that my Federation would like to trade with your—ah, government—but they do not feel that the time is suitable for an approach to our planets by your ships. . . . difficulties of unknown germs and such problems. Therefore, we would like to choose a dead planet which is completely isolated, to meet your ships and exchange cargoes."

This was not a stupid proposal. Bryllw stared at the Terran calculatingly, wondering when the pretense of innocence would cease. The proposition was a practical one for potential enemies. It would be best to agree to it . . . Any extra time they took in negotiating would increase his chances of locating the star systems of the Federation. Also give more time to locate the real captain, for this clown was not speaking for himself, and there had been no time to communicate with the planets of their 'Federation' even if they had been of the nearest star to the two ships. Someone was giving him advice, and that someone knew enough to be valuable, and should be located and kept alive for questioning.

[Ghah! His image of *questioning*. And he likes it!" "No, he doesn't . . . there's no emotion, it's a purely mechanical concept . . . Much as you civilized-type people may not like it, I'm afraid we're going to have to do something about these people. I've got the location of their home planet worked out. With the overcentralization these Authoritarian types have, we can knock them apart with one raid—their subject races could finish the job . . . Uh-oh!" "Nice plans Hahn, but how about plans to survive this little inspection party they've put aboard? We don't seem to be making it."]

Llyllw's voice came into the earphone of Bryllw's helmet as he lumbered after the small group of Terrans who were showing him the ship. He remembered he had left Llyllw in the control room, remembered with difficulty, dragging his mind from a fog of speculations. Llyllw's voice was triumphant.

"A most unfortunate accident seems to have occurred, your Authority . . . I accidentally bumped into the Terran with the weapon. He dropped it, and I most clumsily stepped on it. I am now apologizing profusely. Oh— yes,

I think I see a star chart. It's painted on a bulkhead, and is obviously ornamental, but it looks quite readable."

"Excellent," Bryllw purred into the helmet mike, remembering that this was the officer who had sighted the strange ship and turned on the Infallible without orders. "Of course it is insubordination, punishable by death, to act without orders, unless I officially approve of your action." There was a tense silence from the listener at the other end of the line. Bryllw let him suffer for a moment, then added. "I approve. However, I'll file recommendations that you be promoted—no room for insubordination on the bottom." He added more quietly. "Be ready to seize the control room when I give the signal. Kill the birds, too."

Bryllw turned to the Terran beside him, "Ve thrade, dead planet, stop andh thrade there. I tell my government, it send ships. Where live you people planets? You tell me. I pick out good star between."

Chang smiled. "We have the star maps up in the control room. You mark where your stars are, and our calculating machine will search the records and find the optimum star with unoccupied planets to use as a trade center between us."

Bryllw radiated a mental snarl that rocked the Terran telepaths. The Terrans wanted to know where his home worlds were. Possibly they had invited him to their ship in order to capture and question him. But if something went wrong with the negotiating delegation, and the Captain of the *Wllyll'n* suspected it, he would immediately blast the Terran ship to atoms, and Bryllw with it. It would be the first thing he would decide to do. Bryllw could visualize Captain Rablyn's pleasure at giving the order that would rid him of a Strategic Captain and leave him again master of his own ship.

"Very sorry, Authority and Wise one, but I just trader, arithmetic-doer of trade ship," he said stolidly, knowing he would not be believed. "I not read star maps, not understand where Nll'ni is from here."

Chang looked at him smilingly, a showing of teeth that suddenly seemed deadly. "Perhaps something can be arranged." He turned and stepped through the hatchway into what looked like a machine shop. Spare parts lay around on and under benches.

"Repairs," Chang explained. It was a rather obvious statement but four men were busily working with rapidity and coordination on adjusting an apparatus built into the wall, while a fifth stood by a control chair and aiming device and leaned on a very large red button with one hand. As the others worked they glanced frequently at a viewscreen centered in the apparatus. The screen had two crossed lines quadrasecting it, like a target sighter and firing device. In the center of the screen with the crossed hairs right across the middle of it, was a ship which Bryllw slowly recognized was the *Wllyll'n*.

"Your pardon, Authority," Bryllw walked over and stood by the working men, breathing heavily. They were in easy reach for skull-cracking. "Your pardon, but this appears to be a weapon. Would you explain to me the principle?"

The one holding the button was further away, out of reach, Bryllw noted. He would have to be reached when the others were down.

"Certainly," Chang smiled. "This is our major armament, the Cosmic Regurgitator. It operates upon the Higgledy-Piggledy principle of reciprocal jabberwocky, and can undo the atomic bonds of any object it is focused on. Except of course, large planets and stars—it would only be able to lightly damage a planet for instance, perhaps destroy the atmosphere. There has been considerable speculation among astrophysicists as to what its effect on a star might be. . . . The whingamig here, determines the jabberwocky reciprocal of any object it is set upon, and indicates by different colors —" He waved his hand at a set of rapidly spinning colored lights.

"That color scheme you see, for instance, indicates the jabberwocky reciprocal of your ship. It is unfortunately necessary to focus on something in order to complete certain repairs. The gunners are making test runs on your ship, since it is the nearest large object. There is however, no danger to your ship—that button there, the one that Jukovsky is pressing, keeps the weapon from Regurgitating automatically when it reaches target. Naturally he will be very careful not to let go of it. Let's go into the engine room, shall we?"

Saying nothing, Bryllw looked again at his ship, *Wllyll'n* pictured in the crosshairs of the weapon, and at the Terran lounging, holding down the button with his left hand. He backed off slowly so as not to startle the Terran.

On the way out he made a small gesture to the Nll'nian in a space suit who had been humbly and discreetly following them. "Stay here when I leave," he muttered into the helmet mike. "If there is any trouble, hold down that button!" He looked back at the lumbering slowness of his crewman in the big spacesuit, and the nervous quickness of the Terran who now lounged, facing their way holding down the button and watching the Nll'nian with suspicion. He looked back with gloom. If there were any trouble the *Wllyll'n* would be thoroughly regurgitated. Gloomily he followed Chang into the Engine room.

Chang seated himself on a streamlined plastic housing and cheerfully began to talk. "Now, about the trading. This is a subject on which I am well qualified to negotiate a treaty, due to my Mongol ancestry. We Mongols have always been known for our sympathetic attitude toward traders. However, there remains the problem of overdeveloped and underdeveloped planets, a problem with which I am sure you and your distinguished colleagues are quite familiar, and of course its concomitant problem of the trade of colonial areas with the mother planets, as so admirably explicated by Wilberforce Throckbottom in his magnificent "Ballad of the Boston Tea Party," a work which is regarded by my people as second in excellence only to our own national epic "Tarzan of the Apes." But to return; all these and many other factors must of course be taken into account in any discussion of trade, and I assume you have done so as have we. Therefore, in the light of the aforementioned, we come to a question which might be, and indeed has been by many, regarded as basic —what have you got and what do you want?"

"Well . . . uh . . . we havh rraw materialth of all tybhs . . ."

"So have we."

"Ve havh many industries . . ." Bryllw was cursing mentally. What did this clever clown think he was doing? He remembered the button and shivered. Were they preparing something worse?

"Perhaps something could be arranged there. It also

seems that there might be a possibility of some sort of cultural exchange, such as beads, hatchets and other artifacts."

"What?"

"I said that our exchange would perhaps be most wisely concentrated on manufactured goods of various types to be determined, and on cultural and scientific items, reflecting the various aspects of our two societies."

"Oh, oh yes . . . cultural and . . . er . . . scientific, by all means scientific exchange. Great, uh, mutual benefit." Like that infernal machine in the next room, he thought. Exchange me that! But the Terran was stalling in some way—there was something phony about it all.

[Hahn: "You guys just aren't good liars, that's all."]

"Now as to the planet for trade center . . . I would suggest a dead planet of one of the stars near here. It is, of course, Terran, uh, territory, but we would be glad . . ."

"THE CAT!"

All hands in the engine room came erect and stood respectfully silent. A sleek, black-furred creature, small and walking on all fours, stepped delicately into the compartment, walked about sniffing at the men, climbed to a shelf to look at the viewscreen centered on one of the tubes, ambled about for five minutes or so, then walked out. The men relaxed. One went over and looked at the viewscreen, apparently to be sure everything was all right.

"That was the Chief," said Chang in a low voice. "He takes a look around sometimes to make sure everything's running all right."

"He's quite small," said Bryllw. He should have expected something like this. These Terran clowns had no rank, they were just pretending to be in charge. That creature, whatever else it was, was obviously aware of its own superiority, an officer or better.

["Good thing ol' Strategic Gorilla wasn't in the shop when the cat came in—we had to knock him off a table to keep him out of that electronic mishmash."]

The Terran behind Chang stepped forward and murmured something Bryllw didn't catch. It sounded like "Hooked".

Chang smiled and continued. "Yes. He comes from the oldest intelligent race we have ever encountered, natives of the planet Erewhon. We find their advice invaluable."

Advice? Bryllw thought. Who are they fooling—themselves?

["Nice kitty . . . up here pretty kitty . . . that's it. Go give Chang the word, I've got everything set."]

A Terran appeared in the engineroom hatchway. "The Cat says he is ready to receive the strange beast now."

Bryllw bristled, but he followed the messenger to a small compartment he had not seen before. The damned ship seemed to be honeycombed with all sorts of unlikely places. The room contained a viewscreen and a small bank of control knobs on a black panel, a small bookshelf at one end and a number of satiny cushions scattered about. At first the room seemed to be uninhabited, then he caught a hint of motion in the corner of his eye and whirled.

The Cat was there, looking down at him haughtily from a plastic pillar topped with a velvet cushion.

Bryllw waited for it to speak. The Cat inspected him with an insolent stare, then yawned and looked away with an affectation of indifference, inspecting the viewscreen. The screen showed the control room and his men.

Bryllw realized he was called upon to speak the first word. This creature's manners were no better than those of the High Servants of Erdig. In fact, they were extremely similar . . . well, he had had some experience in dealing with aristocrats, although he looked back on the experience with relief that he had survived. Now he'd have some use for it.

"Excellency and Most Powerful," he began. The Cat's eyes returned to his with some small interest. Encouraged, he continued. "My government when they hear of vast area controlled by your people would like to send a ship with presents, and things for trade, so both our rulers will profit. You ask your slaves tell me where send ship so best trade with your people? This please to you, Wisest Excellency?"

The Cat stretched and yawned delicately, then returned its large luminous eyes to Bryllw. He found their gaze disturbing. The expression was calm, almost fond, filled with confidence too wise to be mere arrogance.

"Qrrrrlw? Prrrup?"

"The Wise One asks if it would please you if he and this ship escorted your ship back to your own home, for he would appreciate meeting more of your admirable species."

The Cat stood up restlessly and looked at the interpreter more anxiously. "Meeerowwwrr, meerowee." After the previous insouciance, the change to concern and pleading aroused Bryllw's cynicism. He watched the Cat suspiciously.

"The Cat wishes to inform you that you need have no fear. No race has lost anything of value by their association with Cats. Cats are most humble and easy to please. They do not take advantage of their superiority and they are not offended if an individual does not accept their advice. Cats are extremely rational."

The Cat rubbed himself against the cushion with an affectionate, almost feminine gesture, looking at Bryllw with large round luminous eyes full of tender concern. It was a wonderful gesture, though perhaps a little bit overdone to be convincing. Bryllw stepped back uneasily, finding an unexpected desire in himself to have some wise and tender creature such as this to give him advice and protect him from the schemes of young and ruthless officers around him.

How could this alien creature of four legs so easily charm him? True, it was a graceful animal, with silky fur that even the most beautiful female of his young adventures would have envied and desired for her own cheeks and shoulders. And of course all aristocrats are trained in tact, having little else to do but converse. It was only typical of aristocrats that this animal had tact. But with a few gestures to give to Bryllw the idea that he would *like* to be ruled by this creature! It must be a lie. Under the velvet paw lay the steel claws—the creature's wisdom and skill were weapons to fear. Bryllw took another step backward and suddenly saw the luminous eyes catch a reflection and flare into lambent wells of green flame. With eyes that radiated light the creature no longer looked like anything real. Fear of hypnosis struck him like a blow, and he looked away from the strange blazing eyes, barely keeping himself from striking out at them or running.

"Qrrmlll. Mrrll meerrowwl." The Cat's voice was close and intimate. The translator's voice seemed far away.

"He says those under his guidance aboard this small ship are very happy due to his wise advice. You can ask any one of them."

This accounted for the smallness of the ship. It was merely a personal pleasure boat for the Cat, manned by his servants. The Terrans were deceiving themselves with their talk of equality and their "Federation". It was no doubt a device of the Cat, trickery to keep them contented.

Suddenly he understood. The Cats were spreading in a great and growing empire of power more absolute than any Bryllw had ever seen, using other species as slaves and keeping them in such hypnotic control that they thought they were free. What need to fear revolt, when the slaves think they are free and are sure they are in charge of their own destiny, merely requesting advice from you?

Bryllw shuddered violently. Thank the Elders he had not sent the regular Captain on this mission. The idiot would have come back bearing the Cat on his shoulder for a "Visit" and they would all have been lost.

"Mrrrr," the Cat said in a low confiding tone, settling down to a couchant position and fixing Bryllw steadily with his large affectionate eyes.

"He wishes to know if he may visit your ship."

Bryllw shuddered in spite of his control. "I will try arrange it," he said, fearful that the Cat would see that he was lying.

The Cat suddenly leaned over and lay on its side looking at the ceiling languidly and said something in a gentle soothing sound like an affectionate growl. The sound evoked youthful memories in the aging Bryllw. He found himself charmed by the tone. Oh, but these aristocrats were charmers always, and masters of tact! But they would kill you without even bothering to get angry.

"He says that his little ship is not fast enough to keep up with yours, and so it would be a favor if you would return home slowly enough to allow him to follow you." The pleasant affectionate growl continued. "He says he admires your fighting spirit and intelligence in understanding his meaning. He has personally taken a fondness to you, and would put you under his protection and do you any favors in his power when his people come into positions of influence in your empire. He is aware by your manner that you are not a trader, but a fighting man of much experience and little scruple, and he might even add you to his personal council."

The Cat still lolled back, staring at the ceiling with a remote and affectionate gaze.

Bryllw, feeling himself to be in the most dangerous crisis of his life, was fascinated. How pleasantly this aristocrat had offered his bribe, how affectionately he had applied the oil and how obliquely shown the dagger!

It would not be safe to say either yes or no. With barely controlled haste he made apologies about diminishing air supply and hurried to the control room. "Come," he growled to the men there, "We're leaving."

"But. . ."

"Shut up and move while you can move! Let's get out of here and never mind asking questions!"

The Terran ship was slower. It would be safer to run than to fight.

Back on board the *Wllyll'n,* Bryllw stalled the Terran over the viewscreen while the ship was made ready for maximum acceleration. Then everything was ready and the *Wllyll'n* suddenly accelerated under full power and departed.

As Bryllw's thoughts blacked out under the bone-crushing acceleration, he was counting himself lucky to have escaped.

Chang sprawled on a lounging pad, wiping his face limply. "I never thought we'd work it. You guys could read his reactions but I had to guess. Diu! I'm beat."

"We all are—never played bluff before. We didn't do it too well. The only one with a good pokerface was Shadow."

"THE CAT!" shouted Hahn. They all leapt to their feet, then relaxed.

"Ahh, cut it out, Hahn."

"Give Shadow his bowl of milk or something."

"How come the Nll'ni don't keep pets?"

"I dunno—how come we *do?*"

A TOUCH OF GRAPEFRUIT

by RICHARD MATHESON

> *Richard Matheson burst like a bright exhalation on the evening with his first published story—a lovely, chilly midget of a yarn called* BORN OF MAN AND WOMAN. *Since then the books have poured out,* THE INCREDIBLE SHRINKING MAN *made motion-picture history, the magazines have been studded with his work. Here is his latest—presenting another facet of Richard Matheson's work, and one you will enjoy.*

Selections from a
*Thesis Submitted as Partial Requirement
For Master of Arts Degree
June, 2068*

The phenomenon known in scientific circles as The Los Angeles Movement came to light in the year 1962 when Doctor Albert Grimsby, A.B., B.S., A.M., Ph.D., professor of physics at the California Institute of Technology made an unusual discovery.

It went like this:

"I have made an unusual discovery," said Doctor Grimsby.

"What is that?" asked Doctor Maxwell.

"Los Angeles is alive."

Doctor Maxwell blinked.

"I beg your pardon," he said.

35

"I can understand your incredulity," said Doctor Grimsby, "Nevertheless . . ."

He drew Doctor Maxwell to the laboratory bench.

"Look into this microscope," he said, "under which I have isolated a piece of Los Angeles."

Doctor Maxwell looked. He raised his head, a look of astonishment on his face.

"It moves," he said.

Having made this strange discovery, Doctor Grimsby— oddly enough—saw fit to promulgate it only in the smallest degree. It appeared as a one-paragraph item in the *Science News Letter* of June 2, 1962 under the heading:

Caltech Physicist Finds
Signs of Life in L.A.

Perhaps due to unfortunate phrasing, perhaps to normal lack of interest, the item aroused neither attention nor comment. This unfortunate negligence proved ever after a plague to the man originally responsible for it. In later years it became known as "Grimsby's Blunder".

Thus was introduced to a then unresponsive nation a phenomenon which was to become, in the following year, a most shocking threat to that nation's very existence.

Of late, researchers have discovered that knowledge concerning The Los Angeles Movement predates Doctor Grimsby's find by years. Indeed, hints of this frightening crisis are to be found in works published as much as fifteen years prior to the ill-fated "Caltech Disclosure".

Concerning Los Angeles, the distinguished journalist, John Gunther, wrote: "What distinguishes it is . . . it's octopus-like growth."[1]

Yet another reference to Los Angeles mentions that: "In its amoeba-like growth it has spread in all directions. . . ."[2]

Thus can be seen primitive approaches to the phenomenon which are as perceptive as they are unaware. Although there is no present evidence to indicate that any person during that early period actually knew of the fantastic process, there can hardly be any doubt that many *sensed* it, if only imperfectly.

[1]John Gunther, *Inside U.S.A.*, p. 44
[2]Henry G. Alsberg (ed.) *The American Guide*, p. 1200

Active speculation regarding freakish nature behavior began in July and August of 1962. During a period of approximately forty-seven days the states of Arizona and Utah, in their entirety, along with great portions of New Mexico and lower Colorado, were inundated by rains that frequently bettered the five-inch mark.

Such waterfall in previously arid sections aroused great agitation and discussion. First theories placed responsibility for this uncommon rainfall on previous southwestern atomic tests.[3] Government disclaiming of this possibility seemed to increase rather than eliminate mass credulity to this later disproved supposition.

Other "precipitation postulations"—as they were then known in investigative parlance can be safely relegated to the category of "crackpotia".[4] These include theories that excess commercial airflights were upsetting the natural balance of the clouds, that deranged Indian rain makers had unwittingly come upon some lethal condensation factor and were applying it beyond all sanity, that strange frost from outer space was seeding Earth's overhead and causing this inordinate precipitation.

And, as seems an inevitable comcomitant to all alien deportment in nature, hypotheses were propounded that this heavy rainfall presaged *Deluge II*. It is clearly recorded that several minor religious groups began hasty construction of "Salvation Arks". One of these arks can still be seen on the outskirts of the small town of Dry Rot, New Mexico, built on a small hill, "still waiting for the flood."[5]

Then came that memorable day when the name of farmer Cyrus Mills became a household word.

"Tarnation!" said farmer Mills.

He gaped in rustic amazement at the object he had come across in his cornfield. He approached it cautiously. He prodded it with a sausage finger.

"Nation," he repeated, less volubly.

Jason Gullwhistle of *The United States Experimental*

[3]Symmes Chadwick, "Will We Drown The World?" *Southwestern Review IV* (Summer 1962) 698 ff.

[4]Guilliame Gaulte, "Les Theories de l'Eau de Ciel Est Cuckoo", *Jaune Journale*, August, 1962

[5]Harry L. Schuler, "Not Long for This world", *South Orange Literary Review*, XL (Sept. 1962) p. 214

Farm Station No. 3, Nebraska, drove his station wagon out to farmer Mills' farm in answer to an urgent phone call. Farmer Mills took Mr. Gullwhistle out to the object.

"That's odd," said Jason Gullwhistle. "It looks like an orange tree."

Close investigation revealed the truth of this remark. It was, indeed, an orange tree.

"Incredible," said Jason Gullwhistle. "An orange tree in the middle of a Nebraska cornfield. I *never.*"

Later they returned to the house for a lemonade and there found Mrs. Mills in halter and shorts, wearing sunglasses and an old chewed-up fur jacket she had exhumed from her crumbling hope chest.

"Think I'll drive into Hollywood," said Mrs. Mills, sixty-five if she was a day.

By nightfall every wire service had embraced the item, and every paper of any prominence whatever had featured it as a humorous insertion on page one.

Within a week, however, the humor had vanished.

Reports came pouring in from every corner of the state of Nebraska, as well as portions of Iowa, Kansas and Colorado—reports of citrus trees discovered in corn and wheat fields, as well as more alarming reports relative to eccentric behavior in the rural populace.

Addiction to the wearing of scanty apparel became noticeable, an inexplicable rise in the sales of frozen orange juice manifested itself and oddly similar letters were received by dozens of chambers of commerce—letters which heatedly demanded the immediate construction of motor speedways, tennis courts, drive-in theatres and drive-in restaurants. And letters which complained of smog.

But it was not until a marked increase in daily temperatures and an equally marked increase of unfathomable citrus tree growth began to imperil the corn and wheat crop that serious action was taken. Local farm groups organized spraying operations but to little or no avail. Orange, lemon and grapefruit trees continued to flourish in geometric proliferation.

And a nation, at long last, became alarmed.

A seminar of the country's top scientists met in Ragweed, Nebraska, the geographical center of this multiplying plague, to discuss possibilities.

"Dynamic tremors in the alluvial sub-strata," said Doctor Kenneth Loam of the University of Denver.

"Mass chemical disorder in soil composition," said Spencer Smith of the duPont Laboratories.

"Momentous gene mutation in the seed corn," said Professor Jeremy Brass of Kansas College.

"Violent contraction of the atmospheric dome," said Professor Lawson Hinkson of M.I.T.

"Displacement of orbit," said Roger Cosmos of the Hayden Planetarium.

"I'm scared," said a little man from Purdue.

Such positive results as may have emerged from this body of speculative genius are yet to be appraised.

History records that a closer labeling of the cause of this unusual behavior in nature and man occurred in early October of 1962, when Associate Professor David Silver, young research physicist at the University of Missouri, published in *The Scientific American* an article entitled, "The Collecting of Evidences."

In this brilliant essay, Professor Silver first voiced the opinion that all the apparently disconnected occurrences were, in actuality, superficial revelations of one underlying phenomenon. To the moment of this article, scant attention had been paid to the erratic behavior of people in the affected areas. Mr. Silver attributed this behavior to the same cause which had effected the alien growth of citrus trees.

The final deductive link was forged, oddly enough, in a Sunday supplement of the now-defunct Hearst newspaper syndicate.[6] The author of this piece, a professional article writer, in doing research for an article, stumbled across the paragraph recounting Doctor Grimsby's discovery. Seeing in this a most salable feature, he wrote an article combining the theses of Doctor Grimsby and Professor Silver and emerging with his own amateur concept which, strange to say, was absolutely correct. (This fact was later obscured in the severe litigation that arose when Professors Grimsby and Silver brought suit against

[6]H. Braham, "Is Los Angeles Alive?", *Los Angeles Sunday Examiner*, October 29, 1962

the author for not consulting them before writing the article.)

Thus did it finally become known that Los Angeles, like some gigantic fungus, was overgrowing the land.

A period of gestation followed during which various publications in the country slowly built up the import of the Los Angeles Movement, until it became a national byword.

It was during this period that a fertile-minded columnist dubbed Los Angeles "Ellie, the Meandering Metropolis," a title later reduced merely to "Ellie"—a term which became as common to the American mind as "ham and eggs" or "World War II."

Now began a cycle of data collection and an attempt by various of the prominent sciences to analyze the Los Angeles movement, with a regard to arresting its strange pilgrimage—which had now spread into parts of South Dakota, Missouri, Arkansas, and as far as the sovereign state of Texas. (Of the mass convulsion this caused in the Lone Star State a separate paper might be devoted.)

REPUBLICANS DEMAND
FULL INVESTIGATION

L.A. Movement Labeled
Subversive Camouflage

After a hasty dispatch of agents to all points in the infected area, the American Medical Association promulgated throughout the nation a list of symptoms by which all inhabitants might be forewarned of the approaching terror:

Symptoms of "Ellieitis"[7]

1. An unnatural craving for any of the citrus fruits, whether in solid or liquid form.
2. Partial or complete loss of geographical distinction. (I.e., a person in Kansas City might speak of driving down to San Diego for the weekend.)
3. An unnatural desire to possess a motor vehicle.

[7]"Ellieitis: Its Symptoms," A.M.A. pamphlet, Fall 1962

4. An unnatural appetite for motion pictures and motion picture previews. (Including a subsidiary symptom, not all-inclusive but never-the-less a distinct menace. This is the insatiable hunger of young girls to become movie stars.)
5. A taste for weird dress apparel. (Including fur jackets, shorts, halters, slacks, sandals, blue jeans and bathing suits—all, usually, of excessive color.)

This list, unfortunately, proved most inadequate for its avowed purpose.

It did not mention, for one thing, the adverse effect of excess sunlight on residents of the northern states. With the expected approach to winter being forestalled indefinitely, numerous unfortunates, unable to adjust to this alteration, became neurotic and, often, lost their senses completely.

The story of Matchbox, North Dakota, a small town in the northernmost part of that state is typical of accounts which flourished throughout the late fall and winter of 1962.

The citizens of this ill-fated town went berserk to a man waiting for the snow and, eventually running amuck, burned their village to the ground.

The pamphlet also failed to mention the psychological phenomenon known later as "Beach Seeking",[8] a delusion under which masses of people, wearing bathing suits and carrying towels and blankets, wandered helplessly across the plains and prairies searching for the Pacific Ocean.

In October, the Los Angeles Movement (the process was given this more staid title in late September by Professor Augustus Wrench in a paper sent to the National Council of American Scientists) picked up momentum. In a space of ten days it engulfed Arkansas, Missouri and Minnesota, and was creeping rapidly into the borderlands of Illinois, Wisconsin, Tennessee, Mississippi and Louisiana.

Smog drifted across the nation.

[8]Fritz Felix Derkatt, "Das Beachen Seeken", *Einzweidrei,* Nov. 1962

Up to this point, citizens on the east coast had been interested in the phenomenon but not overly perturbed, since distance from the diseased territory had lent detachment. Now however, as the Los Angeles city limits stalked closer and closer to them, the coastal region became alarmed.

Legislative activity in Washington was virtually terminated as Congressmen were inundated with letters of protest and demand. A special committee, heretofore burdened by general public apathy in the east, now became enlarged by the added membership of several distinguished Congressmen. A costly probe into the problem ensued.

It was this committee that, during the course of its televised hearings, unearthed a secret group known as the *L.A. Firsters*.

This insidious organization seemed to have sprung almost spontaneously from the general chaos of the Los Angeles envelopment. General credence was given for a short time to the idea that it was another symptom of "Ellieitis". Intense interrogation, however, revealed the existence of *L.A. Firster* cells in east-coast cities that could not possibly have been subject to the dread virus at that point.

This revelation struck terror into the heart of a nation. The presence of such calculated subversion in this moment of trial almost unnerved the national will. For it was not merely an organization loosely joined by emotional binds. This faction possessed a carefully wrought hierarchy of men and women, plotting the overthrow of the national government. Nationwide distribution of literature had begun almost with the advent of the Los Angeles Movement. This literature, with the cunning of insurgent casuistry, painted a roseate picture of the future of—the United States of Los Angeles!

PEOPLE ARISE![9]

People arise! Cast off the shackles of reaction! What sense is there in opposing the march of PROG-

[9]*The Los Angeles Manifesto*, L.A. Firster Press, Winter, 1962

RESS! It is inevitable! And you, the people of this glorious land—a land dearly bought with *your* blood and *your* tears—should realize that *Nature herself!* supports the L.A. FIRSTERS!

How?—you ask. How does Nature support this glorious adventure?

The question is simple enough to answer.

NATURE HAS SUPPORTED THE L.A. FIRSTER MOVEMENT FOR THE BETTERMENT OF *YOU*!

Here are a few facts. In those states that have been blessed:

1. Rheumatism has dropped 52%,
2. Pneumonia has dropped 61%,
3. Frostbite has *vanished,*
4. Incidence of the COMMON COLD has dropped 73%!

Is this bad news? Are these the changes brought about by anti-PROGRESS?

NO!!!

Wherever Los Angeles has gone, the deserts have fled, adding millions of new fertile acres to our beloved land. Where once there was only sand and catcus and *bleached bones* are now plants and trees and FLOWERS!

This pamphlet closes with a couplet which aroused a nation to fury:

> *Sing out O land, with flag unfurled!*
> *Los Angeles! Tomorrow's World!*

The exposure of the L.A. Firsters caused a tide of reaction to sweep the city.

Rage became the keynote of this counter-revolution; rage at the subtlety with which the L.A. Firsters had distorted truth in their literature; rage at their arrogant assumption that the country would inevitably fall to Los Angeles.

Slogans of "Down with the L.A. Lovers!" and "Send Them Back Where They Came from!" rang throughout the land. A measure was forced through Congress and got the presidential signature, outlawing the group and making membership in it the offense of treason. Rabid groups attached a rider to this measure which would have enforced the outlawry, seizure and destruction of all tennis and beach-supply manufacturing. Here, however, the N.A.M. stepped into the scene and, through the judicious use of various pressure means, defeated the attempt.

Despite this quick retaliation, the L.A. Firsters continued underground, and at least one fatality of its persistent agitation was the state of Missouri.

In some manner, as yet undisclosed, the L.A. Firsters gained control of the state legislature and jockeyed through an amendment to the constitution of Missouri which was hastily ratified and made the Show-Me state the first area in the country to legally make itself a part of Los Angeles County.

UTTER McKINLEY OPENS
FIVE NEW PARLORS
IN THE SOUTHWEST

In the succeeding months there emerged a notable upsurge in the production of automobiles, particularly convertibles. In those states affected by the Los Angeles Movement every citizen, apparently, had acquired that symptom of "Ellieitis" known as *automania*. The car industry entered accordingly upon a period of peak production, its factories turning out automobiles twenty-four hours a day, seven days a week.

In conjunction with this increase in automotive fabrication there began a near-maniacal splurge in the building of drive-in restaurants and theatres. These sprang up with mushroomlike celerity through western and midwestern United States, their planning going beyond all feasibility. Typical of these thoughtless projects was the endeavor to hollow out a mountain and convert it into a drive-in theatre.[10]

As the month of December approached, the Los Angeles Movement engulfed Illinois, Wisconsin, Mississippi, half of Tennessee and was lapping at the shores of Indiana, Kentucky and Alabama. (No mention will be made of the profound effect this movement had on racial seg-

---

[10]L. Savage, "A Report on The Grand Teton Drive-In", *Fortune*, January, 1963

regation in the South, this subject demanding a complete investigation in itself.)

It was about this time that a wave of religious passion obsessed the nation.

As is the nature of the human mind suffering catastrophe, millions turned to religion. Various cults had, in this calamity, grist for their metaphysical mills.

Typical of these were *The San Bernadino Vine Worshipers,* who claimed Los Angeles to be the reincarnation of their deity *Ochsalia*—The Vine Divine. *The San Diego Sons of the Weed* claimed, in turn, that Los Angeles was a sister embodiment to their deity which they claimed had been creeping for three decades prior to the Los Angeles Movement.

Unfortunately for all concerned, a small fascistic clique began to usurp control of many of these otherwise harmless cults, emphasizing dominance through "power and energy."

As a result, these religious bodies too often degenerated into mere fronts for political cells that plotted the overthrow of the government for purposes of self-aggrandizement. (Secret documents discovered in later years revealed the intention of one perfidious brotherhood of converting the Pentagon Building into an indoor race track.)

During a period beginning in September and extending for years, there also ensued a studied expansion of the motion-picture industry. Various of the major producers opened branch studios throughout the country. For example, M-G-M built one in Terre Haute, R.K.O. Radio in Cincinnati and Twentieth Century-Fox in Tulsa. The Screen Writer's Guild initiated branch offices in every large city, and the term "Hollywood" became even more of a misnomer than it had previously been.

Motion-picture output more than quadrupled, as theaters of all description were hastily erected everywhere west of the Mississippi, sometimes wall-to-wall for blocks.[11] These buildings were rarely well constructed, and often collapsed within weeks of their "grand openings."

Yet, in spite of the incredible number of theaters, mo-

[11]"Gulls Creek Gets Its Forty Eighth Theatre", *The Arkansas Post-Journal,* March 12, 1963

tion pictures exceeded them in quantity (if not quality). It was in compensation for this economically dangerous situation that the studios inaugurated the expedient practice of burning films in order to maintain the stability of the price floor. This aroused great antipathy among the smaller studios who did not produce enough films to burn any.

Another liability involved in the production of motion pictures was the geometric increase in difficulties raised by small but voluble pressure groups.

One typical coterie was *The Anti-Horse League* of Dallas, which put up strenuous opposition to the utilization of horses in films.

This, plus the increasing incidence of car-owning which had made horse breeding unprofitable, made the production of Western films (as they had been known) an impossible chore. Thus was it that the so-called "Western" gravitated rapidly toward the "drawing-room" drama.

Section of a Typical Screenplay[12]

Tex D'Urberville comes riding into Doomtown on the Colorado, his Jaguar raising a cloud of dust in the sleepy western town. He parks in front of the Golden Sovereign Saloon and steps out. He is a tall, rangy cowhand impeccably attired in waistcoat and fawnskin trousers with a ten-gallon hat, boots and pearl-gray spats. A heavy six-gun is belted at his waist. He carries a gold-topped malacca cane.

He enters the saloon. Every man there scatters from the room, leaving only Tex and a scowling hulk of a man at the other end of the bar. This is Dirty Ned Updyke, local ruffian and gunman.

TEX: (Removing his white gloves and, pretending he does not see Dirty Ned, addressing the bartender) Pour me a whiskey and seltzer, will you, Roger, there's a good fellow.

[12]Maxwell Brande, "Altercation at Deadwood Spa", Epigram Studios, April, 1963

ROGER: Yes, sir.

Dirty Ned scowls over his aperitif but does not dare to reach for the Webley Automatic pistol which is concealed in a holster beneath his tweed jacket.

Now Tex D'Urberville allows his icy blue eyes to move slowly about the room until they rest on the craven features of Dirty Ned.

TEX: So . . . you're the beastly cad who shot my brother.

Instantly they draw their cane swords and, approaching, salute each other grimly.

An additional result not to be overlooked was the effect of increased film production on politics. The need for high salaried workers such as writers, actors, directors and plumbers was intense. This mass of nouveau riche, having come upon good times so relatively abruptly, acquired a definite guilt neurosis which resulted in their intensive participation in the so-called "liberal" and "progressive" groups. This swelling of radical activity did much to alter the course of American political history. (This subject being another which requires separate inquiry for a proper evaluation of its many and varied ramifications.)

Two other factors of this period which may be mentioned briefly are the increase in divorce due to the relaxation of divorce laws in every state affected by the Los Angeles Movement and the slow but eventually complete bans placed upon tennis and beach supplies by a rabid but powerful group within the N.A.M. This ban led, inexorably, to a brief span of time which paralleled the so-called "Prohibition" period of the 1920's. During this infamous period, thrill seekers attended the many bootleg tennis courts throughout the country, which sprang up wherever perverse public demand made them profitable ventures for unscrupulous men.

In the first days of January, 1963, the Los Angeles Movement reached almost to the Atlantic shoreline.

Panic spread through New England and the southern coastal region. The country and, ultimately, Washington reverberated with cries of *"Stop Los Angeles!"* All processes of government ground to a virtual halt in the ensuing chaos.

Law enforcement atrophied, crime waves spilled across the nation and conditions became so grave that even the outlawed L.A. Firsters held revival meetings in the streets.

ABOUTOWN WITH PULLEY[13]

Just got in from a little town in Pennsylvania called Dutch Corners where I talked to a member of the outlawed L.A. Firsters. Here are some of the things that were said:

Q. You think L.A. will cover the country?

A. Sure will, brother! It'll cover the Earth!

Q. What about the destruction of the grain crop by citrus trees?

A. So we'll eat oranges, brother! Oranges are good for you.

Q. But what about bread?

A. Let 'em eat cake, brother, let 'em eat cake!

Q. So you think it's a good thing.

A. Sure, it's a good thing. Why, on a clear day you can see Catalina!

On February 11, 1963, the Los Angeles Movement forded the Hudson River and invaded Manhattan Island.

Flame-throwing tanks proved futile against the invincible flux. Within a week the subways were closed and car purchases had trebled. Within two years New York had joined The Federation of Los Angeles, and had become obliged to saw off all its skyscrapers in order to adhere to the Los Angeles building code, which prescribed heights of no more than 150 feet. (The trimmings were given to Brooklyn.)

By March, 1963, the only unaltered states in the union were Maine, Vermont, New Hampshire and Massachusetts. This was later explained by the lethargic adaptation of the fungi to the rocky New England soil and inclement weather.

[13]Column by Eastbrook Pulley, *New York Daily Mirror*, January 7, 1963

These northern states, cornered and helpless, resorted to extraordinary measures in a hopeless bid to ward off the awful incrustation. Several of them legalized the mercy killing of any person discovered to have acquired the taint of "Ellieitis." Newspaper reports of shootings, stabbings, poisonings and strangulations became so common in those days of "The Last-Ditch Defense" that newspapers inaugurated a daily section of its contents to such reports.

Boston, Mass. April 13, AP—Last rites were held today for Mr. Abner Scrounge who was shot after being found in his garage, attempting to remove the top of his Rolls Royce with a can opener.

The history of the gallant battle of Boston to retain its essential dignity would, alone, make up a large work. The story of how the intrepid citizens of this venerable city refused to surrender their rights, choosing mass suicide rather than submission is a tale of enduring courage and majestic struggle against insurmountable odds.

What happened after the movement was contained within the boundaries of the United States (a name soon discarded) is data for another paper.

A brief mention, however, may be made of the immense social endeavor which became known as the "Bacon and Waffles" movement, which sought to guarantee $250 per month for every person in Los Angeles over forty years of age.

With this incentive before the people, state legislatures were helpless before an avalanche of public demand. Within three years, the entire nation was a part of Los Angeles. The government seat was in Beverly Hills and ambassadors had been hastened to all foreign countries within a short period of time.

Ten years later the North American continent fell, and Los Angeles was creeping rapidly down the Isthmus of Panama. Then came that ill-fated day in 1974.

On the island of Pingo Pongo, Maona, daughter of Chief Luana approached her father.

"Omu la golu si mongo?" she said.

(Anyone for tennis?)

Whereupon her father, having read the papers, speared her on the spot and ran screaming from the hut.

COMPANY STORE

by ROBERT SILVERBERG

Robert Silverberg does not type with his toes as well as both hands, it only seems that way. Certainly few science-fiction writers, old or new, can match the incomparable productivity of this bright young star in STAR's firmament. He has mastered the men's adventure field, the general magazines and nearly every other facet of the writing world; but always he comes back to science fiction— where stories like COMPANY STORE make him eternally welcome.

Colonist Roy Wingert gripped his blaster with shaky hands. He took dead aim at the slimy wormlike creatures wriggling behind his newly-deposited pile of crates.

They told me this planet was uninhabited, he thought. *Hah!*

He yanked back the firing stud. A spurt of violet light leaped out.

His nostrils caught the smell of roasting alien flesh. Shuddering, Wingert turned away from the mess before him, in time to see four more of the wormlike beings writhing toward him from the rear.

He ashed those. Two more dangled invitingly from a thick-boled tree at his left.

Getting into the spirit of the thing now, Wingert turned the beam on them, too. The clearing was beginning to look like the vestibule of an abattoir. Sweat ran down

Wingert's face. His stomach was starting to get queasy, and his skin was cold at the prospect of spending his three-year tour on Quellac doing nothing but fighting off these overgrown night-crawlers.

Two more of them were wriggling out of a decaying log near his feet. They were nearly six feet long, with saw-edged teeth glistening in Quellac's bright sunlight. *Nothing very dangerous,* Wingert thought grimly. *Ho!* He recharged the blaster and roasted the two newcomers.

Loud noises back of him persuaded him to turn. Something very much like a large gray toad, seven or eight feet high and mostly mouth, was hopping toward him through the forest. It was about thirty yards away now. It looked very hungry.

Squaring his shoulders, Wingert prepared to defend himself against this new assault. But just as he started to depress the firing stud, a motion to his far right registered in the corner of his eye. *Another* of the things—approaching rapidly from the opposite direction.

"Pardon me, sir," a sharp crackling voice said suddenly. "You seem to be in serious straits. May I offer you the use of this Duarm Pocket Force-Field Generator in this emergency? The cost is only—"

Wingert gasped. *"Damn* the cost! Turn the thing on! Those toads are only twenty feet away!"

"Of course, sir."

Wingert heard a click, and abruptly a shimmering blue bubble of force sprang up around them. The two onrushing pseudo-toads cracked soundly into it and were thrown back.

Wingert staggered over to one of the packing-cases and sat down limply. He was soaked with sweat from head to foot.

"Thanks," he said. "You saved my life. But who the hell are you, and where'd you come from?"

"Permit me to introduce myself. I am XL-ad41, a new-model Vending and Distributing Robot manufactured on Densobol II. I arrived here not long ago, and, perceiving your plight—"

Wingert saw now that the creature was indeed a robot, roughly humanoid except for a heavy pair of locomotory treads. "Hold on! Let's go back to the beginning." The toad-things were eyeing him hungrily from outside the force-field. "You say you're a new-model *what?*"

"Vending and Distributing Robot. It is my function to diffuse through the civilized galaxy the goods and supplies manufactured by my creators, Associated Artisans of Densobol II." The robot's rubberized lips split in an oily smile. "I am, you might say, a mechanized Traveling Salesman. Are you from Terra, perhaps?"

"Yes, but—"

"I thought as much. By comparing your physical appearance with the phenotype data in my memory banks I reached the conclusion that you were of Terra origin. The confirmation you have just given is most gratifying."

"Glad to hear it. Densobol II is in the Magellanic Cluster, isn't it? Lesser or Greater Cloud?"

"Lesser. One matter puzzles me, though. In view of your Terran origin, it seems odd that you didn't respond when I mentioned that I am a traveling salesman."

Wingert frowned. "How was I supposed to respond? Clap my hands and wriggle my ears?"

"You were supposed to show humor-response. According to my files on Terra, mention of traveling salesmen customarily strikes upon a common well of folklore implanted in the subconscious, thereby inducing a conscious humor-reaction."

"Sorry," Wingert apologized. "I'm afraid I never was too interested in Earth. That's why I signed on with Planetary Colonization."

"Ah, yes. I had just concluded that your failure to show response to standard folklore indicated some fundamental dislocation of your position relative to your cultural *gestalt*. Again, confirmation is gratifying. As an experimental model, I'm subject to careful monitoring by my makers. I'm anxious to demonstrate my capability as a salesman."

Wingert had almost completely recovered from his earlier exertions. He eyed the two toad-beings uneasily and said, "That force-field generator—that's one of the things you sell?"

"The Duarm Generator is one of our finest products. It's strictly one-way, you know. *They* can't get in, but you can still fire at them."

"What? Why didn't you tell me that long ago?" Wingert

drew his blaster and disposed of the toad-creatures with two well-placed shots.

"That's that," he said. "I guess I sit inside this force-field and wait for the next ones, now."

"Oh, they won't be along for a while," the robot said lightly. "The creatures that attacked you are native to the next continent. They're not found here at all."

"Then how'd they get here?"

"I brought them," the robot said sunnily. "I collected the most hostile creatures I could find on this world, and left them in your vicinity in order to demonstrate the necessity for the Duarm Force-Field Generat—"

"*You* brought them?" Wingert rose and advanced on the robot menacingly. "Deliberately, as a sales stunt? They could have killed and eaten me!"

"On the contrary. I was controlling the situation, as you saw. When matters became serious I intervened."

"Get out of here!" Wingert raged. "Go on, you crazy robot! I have to set up my bubble. Go!"

"But you owe me—"

"We'll settle up later. Get going, *fast!*"

The robot got. Wingert watched it scuttle off into the underbrush.

He tried to control his rage. Angry as he was, he felt a certain amusement at the robot's crude sales-tactics. It was clever, in a coarse way, to assemble a collection of menacing aliens and arrive at the last minute to supply the force-field. But when you poison a man in order to sell him the antidote, you *don't* boast about it afterward to the victim!

He glanced speculatively at the forest, hoping the robot had told the truth. He didn't care to spend his entire tour on Quellac fighting off dangerous beasts.

The generator was still operating; Wingert studied it and found a cam that widened the field. He expanded it to a thirty-yard radius and left it that way. The clearing was littered with alien corpses.

Wingert shuddered.

Well, now that amusement was over, it was time to get down to business. He had been on Quellac just an hour, and had spent most of that time fighting for his life.

The Colonists' Manual said, *"The first step for a newly-arrived colonist is to install his Matter-Transmitter."*

Wingert closed the book and peered at the scattered pile of crates that were his possessions until he spied the large yellow box labeled *Matter-Transmitter, Handle With Care*.

From the box marked *Tools* he took a crowbar and delicately pried a couple of planks out of the packing-crate. A silvery metallic object was visible within. Wingert hoped the Matter-Transmitter was in working order; it was his most important possession, his sole link to far-off Terra.

The Manual said, *"All necessities of life will be sent via matter-transmitter without cost."* Wingert smiled. Necessities of life? He could have magneboots, cigars, senso tapes, low-power short-range matter-transmitters, dream pellets, bottled Martinis and nuclear fizzes, simply by requisitioning them. All the comforts of home. They had told him working for Planetary Colonization was rugged, but it was hardly that. Not with the Matter-Transmitter to take the sting out of pioneering.

Unless, Winger thought gloomily, *that lunatic robot brings some more giant toads over from the next continent.*

Wingert opened the packing crate and bared the Matter-Transmitter. It looked, he thought, like an office-desk with elephantiasis of the side drawers; they bulged grotesquely, aproning out into shovel-shaped platforms, one labeled *"Send"* and the other *"Receive."*

An imposing-looking array of dials and meters completed the machine's face. Wingert located the red Activator Stud along the north perimeter and jammed it down.

The Matter-Transmitter came quiveringly to life.

Dials clicked; meters registered. The squarish device seemed to have taken on existence of its own. The view-screen flickered polychromatically, then cleared.

A mild pudgy face stared out at Wingert.

"Hello. I'm Smathers, from the Earth Office. I'm the company contact man for Transmitters AZ-1061 right through BF-80. Can I have your name, registry number, and coordinates?"

"Roy Wingert, Number 76-032-10f3. The name of this planet is Quellac, and I don't know the coordinates off-hand. If you'll give me a minute to check my contract—"

"No need of that," Smathers said. "Just let me have

the serial number of your Matter-Transmitter. It's inscribed on the plate along the west perimeter."

Wingert found it after a moment's search. "AZ-1142."

"That checks. Well, welcome to the Company, Colonist Wingert. How's your planet?"

"Not so good," Wingert said.

"How so?"

"It's inhabited. By hostile aliens. And my contract said I was being sent to an uninhabited world."

"Read it again, Colonist Wingert. As I recall, it simply said you would meet no hostile creatures where *you* were. Our survey team reported some difficulties on the wild continent to your west, but—"

"You see these dead things here?"

"Yes."

"I killed them. To save my own neck. They attacked me about a minute after the Company ship dropped me off here."

"They're obviously strays from that other continent," Smathers said. "Most unusual. Be sure to report any further difficulties of this sort."

"Sure," Wingert said. "Big comfort *that* is."

"To change the subject," Smathers said frigidly, "I wish to remind you that the Company stands ready to serve you. In the words of the contract, '*All necessities of life will be sent via Matter-Transmitter.*' That's in the Manual too. Would you care to make your first order now? The Company is extremely anxious that its employees are well taken care of."

Wingert frowned. "Well, I haven't even unpacked, you know. I don't think I need anything yet—except—yes! Send me some old-fashioned razor-blades, will you? And a tube of shaving cream. I forgot to pack mine in, and I can't stand these new vibro-shaves."

Smathers emitted a suppressed chuckle. "You're not going to grow a beard?"

"No," Wingert said stiffly. "They itch."

"Very well, then. I'll have the routing desk ship a supply of blades and cream to Machine AZ-1142. So long for now, Colonist Wingert, and good luck. The Company sends its best wishes."

"Thanks," Wingert said sourly. "Same to you."

He turned away from the blank screen and glanced beyond the confines of his force-field. All seemed quiet, so he snapped off the generator.

Quellac, he thought, had the makings of a darned fine world, except for the beasts on the western continent. The planet was Earth-type, sixth in orbit around a small yellow main-sequence star. The soil was red with iron-salts, but looked fertile enough, judging from the thick vegetation pushing up all around. Not far away a sluggish little stream wound through a sloping valley and vanished in a hazy cloud of purple mist near the horizon.

It would be a soft enough life, he thought, if no more toads showed up. Or worms with teeth.

The contract specified that his job was to "prepare and otherwise survey the world assigned, for the purpose of admitting future colonists under the auspices of Planetary Colonization, Inc." He was an advance agent, sent out by the Company to smooth the bugs out of the planet before the regular colonists arrived.

For this they gave him $1,000 a month, plus "necessities of life" via Matter-Transmitter.

There were worse ways of making a living, Wingert told himself.

A lazy green-edged cloud was drifting over the forest. He pushed aside a blackened alien husk and sprawled out on the warm red soil, leaning against the Matter-Transmitter's comforting bulk. Before him were the eight or nine crates containing his equipment and possessions.

He had made the three-week journey from Earth to Quellac aboard the first-class liner *Mogred*. Matter-transmission would have been faster, but a Transmitter could handle a bulk of 150 pounds, which was Wingert's weight, only in three 50-pound installments. That idea didn't appeal to him. Besides, there had been no Matter-Transmitter set up on Quellac to receive him, which made the whole problem fairly academic.

A bird sang softly. Wingert yawned. It was early afternoon, and he didn't feel impatient to set up his shelter. The Manual said it took but an hour to unpack. Later, then, when the sun was sinking behind those cerise mountains, he would blow his bubble-home and unpack his goods. Right now he just wanted to relax, to let the tension of that first fierce encounter drain away.

"Pardon me, sir," said a familiar sharp voice. "I happened to overhear that order for razor blades, and I think it's only fair to inform you that I carry a product of much greater face-appeal."

Wingert was on his feet in an instant, glaring at the robot. "I told you to go away. A-W-A-Y."

Undisturbed, the robot produced a small translucent tube filled with a glossy green paste. "This," XL-ad41 said, "is Gloglam's Depilating Fluid, twelve units—ah, one dollar, that is—per tube."

Wingert shook his head. "I get my goods free, from Terra. Besides, I like to shave with a razor. *Please* go away."

The robot looked about as crestfallen as a robot could possibly look. "You don't seem to understand that your refusal to purchase from me reflects adversely on my abilities, and may result in my being dismantled at the end of this test. Therefore I insist you approach my merchandise with an open mind."

A sudden grin of salesman-like inspiration illuminated XL-ad41's face. "I'll take the liberty of offering you this free sample. Try Gloglam's Depilating Fluid and I can guarantee you'll never use a blade-razor again."

The robot poured a small quantity of the green fluid into a smaller vial and handed it to Wingert. "Here. I'll return shortly to hear your decision."

The robot departed, trampling down the shrubbery with its massive treads. Wingert scratched his stubbly chin and regarded the vial quizzically.

Gloglam's Depilating Fluid, eh? And XL-ad41, the robot traveling salesman. He smiled wryly. On Earth they bombarded you with singing commercials, and here in the wilds of deep space robots from Densobol came descending on you trying to sell shaving-cream.

Well, if the robot salesman were anything like its Terran counterparts, the only way he'd be able to get rid of it would be by buying something from it. And particularly since the poor robot seemed to be on a trial run, and might be destroyed if it didn't make sales. As a one-time salesman himself, Wingert felt sympathy.

Cautiously he squeezed a couple of drops of Gloglam's Depilating Fluid into his palm and rubbed it against one cheek. The stuff was cool and slightly sharp, with a pleasant twang. He rubbed it in for a moment, wondering if it might be going to dissolve his jawbone, then pulled out his pocket mirror.

His face was neat and pink where he'd applied the depilator. He hadn't had such a good shave in years. Enthusiastically he rubbed the remainder of the tube on his face, thereby discovering that the robot had given him just enough to shave one cheek and most of his chin.

Wingert chuckled. Bumbling and pedantic it might be, but the creature knew a little basic salesmanship, at least.

"Well?" XL-ad41 asked, reappearing as if beckoned. "Are you satisfied?"

Grinning, Wingert said, "That was pretty sly—giving me enough to shave half my face, I mean. But the stuff is good; there's no denying that."

"How many tubes will you take?"

Wingert pulled out his billfold. He had brought only $16 with him; he hadn't expected to have any use for Terran currency on Quellac, but there had been a ten, a five, and a one in his wallet at blastoff time.

"One tube," he said. He handed the robot the tattered single. XL-ad41 bowed courteously, reached into a pectoral compartment, and drew out the remainder of the tube he had shown Wingert before.

"Uh-uh," the Earthman said quickly. "That's the tube you took the sample from—and the sample was supposed to be free. I want a full tube."

"The proverbial innate shrewdness of the Terran," XL-ad41 observed mournfully. "I defer to it."

It gave a second tube to Wingert, who examined it and slid it into his tunic. "And now, if you'll excuse me, I have some unpacking to do," Wingert said.

He strode around the smiling robot, grabbed the crowbar, and began opening the crate that housed his bubble-home. Suddenly the Matter-Transmitter emitted a series of loud buzzes followed by a dull *clonk*.

"Your machine has delivered something," XL-ad41 ventured.

Wingert lifted the lid of the *"Receive"* platform and drew out a small package wrapped neatly in plastofil. He peeled away the wrapping.

Within was a box containing twenty-four double-edged blades, a tube of shaving cream, and a bill folded lengthwise. Wingert read it:

Razor blades, as ordered $00.23
Shaving cream, as ordered.................. 00.77
Charge for transportation................... 50.00

Total........$51.00

"You look pale," the robot said. "Perhaps you have some disease. You might be interested in purchasing the Derblong Self-Calibrating Medical Autodiagnostical Servo-mechanism, which I happen to—"

"No," Wingert said grimly. "I don't need anything like that. Get out of my way."

He stalked back to the Transmitter and jabbed down savagely on the Activator Stud. A moment later Smathers' bland voice said, "Hello, Colonist Wingert. Something wrong?"

"There sure is," Wingert said in a strangled voice. "My razor-blades just showed up—with a $50 bill for transportation! What kind of racket is this, anyway? I was told that you'd ship my supplies out free of charge. It says in the contract—"

"The contract says," Smathers interrupted smoothly, "that all necessities of life will be transmitted without cost, Colonist Wingert. It makes no mention of free supply of luxuries. The Company would be unable to bear the crushing financial burden of transporting any and all luxury items a colonist might desire."

"Razor blades are luxury items?" Wingert choked back an impulse to kick the Transmitter's control-panel in. "How can you have the audacity to call razor blades *luxury items?*"

"Most colonists let their beards grow," Smathers said. "Your reluctance to do so, Colonist Wingert, is your own affair. The Company—"

"I know. The Company cannot be expected to bear the crushing financial burden. Okay," Wingert said. "In the future I'll be more careful about what I order. And as for now, take these damned razor blades back and cancel the requisition." He dumped the package in the *"Send"* bin and depressed the control stud.

"I'm sorry you did that," Smathers said. "It will now be necessary for us to assess you an additional $50 to cover return shipping."

"What?"

"However," Smathers went on, "we'll see to it after this that you're notified in advance any time there may be a shipping charge on goods sent to you."

"Thanks," Wingert said hoarsely.

"Since you don't want razor blades, I presume you're going to grow a beard. I rather thought you would. Most colonists do, you know."

"I'm not growing any beards. Some vending robot from the Densobol system wandered through here about ten minutes ago and sold me a tube of depilating paste."

Smathers' eyes nearly popped. "You'll have to cancel that purchase," he said, his voice suddenly stern.

Wingert stared incredulously at the pudgy face in the screen. "Now you're going to interfere with that, *too?*"

"Purchasing supplies from anyone but the Company is a gross violation of your Contract, Colonist Wingert! It makes you subject to heavy penalty! After all, we agreed to supply you with your needs. For you to call in an outside supplier is to rob the Company of its privilege of serving you, Colonist Wingert. You see?"

Wingert was silent for almost a minute, too dizzy with rage to frame his words. Finally he said, "So I get charged $50 shipping costs every time I requisition razor blades from you people, but if I try to buy depilating paste on my own it violates my contract? Why, that's—that's usury! Slavery! It's illegal!"

The voice from the Matter-Transmitter coughed warningly. "Powerful accusations, Colonist Wingert. I suggest that before you hurl any more abuse at the Company you read your contract more carefully."

"I don't give a damn about the contract! I'll buy anywhere I please!"

Smathers grinned triumphantly. "I was afraid you'd say that. You realize that you've now given us legal provocation to slap a spybeam on you in order to make sure you don't cheat us by violating your contract?"

Wingert sputtered. "Spybeam? But—I'll smash your accursed Transmitter! *Then* try to spy on me!"

"We won't be able to," Smathers conceded. "But destroying a Transmitter is a serious felony, punishable by heavy fine. Good afternoon, Colonist Wingert."

"Hey! Come back here! You can't—"

Wingert punched the Activator Stud three times, but Smathers had broken the contact and would not re-open it.

Scowling, Wingert turned away and sat down on the edge of a crate.

"Can I offer you a box of Sugrath Anti-Choler Tranquilizing Pills?" XL-ad41 said helpfully. "Large economy size."

"Shut up and leave me alone!"

Wingert stared moodily at the shiny tips of his boots. The Company, he thought, had him sewed up neatly. He had no money and no way of returning to Earth short of dividing himself into three equal chunks and teleporting. And though Quellac was an attractive planet, it lacked certain aspects of Earth. Tobacco, for one. Wingert enjoyed smoking.

A box of cigars would be $2.40 plus $75 shipping-costs. And Smathers would smirk and tell him cigars were luxuries.

Sensotapes? Luxuries. Short-range transmitters? Maybe those came under the contract, since they were tools. But the pattern was clear. By the time his three-year tour was up, there would be $36,000 in salary waiting in his account—minus the various accumulated charges. He'd be lucky if he came out owing less than $20,000.

Naturally, he wouldn't have that sort of money, and so the benevolent Company would offer a choice: either go to jail or take another three-year term to pay off your debt. So they'd ship him some place else, and at the end of that time he'd be in twice as deep.

Year after year he would sink further into debt, thanks to that damnable contract. He'd spend the rest of his life opening up new planets for Planetary Colonizations, Inc., and never have anything to show for it but a staggering debt.

It was worse than slavery.

There had to be some way out.

But after ransacking the contract for nearly an hour, Wingert concluded that it was airtight.

Angrily he glared up at the beaming robot.

"What are you hanging around here for? You've made your sale. Shove off!"

XL-ad41 shook its head. "You still owe me $500 for

the generator. And surely you can't expect me to return to my manufacturers after having made only two sales. Why, they'd turn me off in an instant and begin developing an XL-ad42!"

"Did you hear what Smathers said? I'll be violating my contract if they see me buying anything more from you. Go on, now. Take your generator back. The sale is cancelled. Visit some other planet; I'm in enough hot water as it is without—"

"Sorry," the robot said, and it seemed to Wingert that there was an ominous note in its mellow voice. "This is the seventeenth planet I've called at since being sent forth by my manufacturers, and I have no sale to show for it but one tube of Gloglam Depilating Fluid. It's a poor record. I don't dare return yet."

"Try somewhere else, then. Find a planet full of suckers and give 'em the hard sell. I can't buy from you."

"I'm afraid you'll have to," the robot said mildly. "My specifications call for me to return to Densobol for inspection after my seventeenth visit." A panel in the robot's abdomen opened whirringly and Wingert saw the snout of a Molecular Disruptor emerge.

"The ultimate sales-tactic, eh? If the customer won't buy, pull a gun and *make* him buy. Except it won't work here. I haven't any money."

"Your friends on Terra will send some. I *must* return to Densobol with a successful sales record. Otherwise—"

"I know. They'll dismantle you."

"Correct. Therefore, I must approach you this way. And I fully intend to carry out my threat if you refuse."

"Hold on here!" a new voice cut in. "What's going on, Wingert?"

Wingert glanced at the Transmitter. The screen was lit, and Smathers' plump face glared outward at him.

"It's this robot," Wingert said. "It's under some sort of sales-compulsion, and it just pulled a gun on me."

"I know. I saw the whole thing on the spybeam."

"I'm in a nice spot now," Wingert said dismally. He glanced from the waiting robot to the unsmiling Smathers. "If I don't buy from this robot, it'll murder me—and if I *do* buy anything, you'll spy it and fine me." Wingert wondered vaguely which would be worse.

"I stock many fine devices unknown on earth," the robot said proudly. "A Pioneer-Model Dreeg-Skinner, in case there are dreegs on Quellac—though frankly I doubt that. Or else you might want our Rotary Diatom-Strainer, or perhaps a new-model Hegley Neuronic Extractor—"

"Quiet," Wingert snapped. He turned back to Smathers. "Well, what do I do? You're the Company; protect your colonist from this marauding alien."

"We'll send you a weapon, Colonist Wingert."

"And have me try to outdraw a robot? You're a lot of help," Wingert said broodingly. Even if he escaped somehow from this dilemma, he knew the Company still had him by the throat over the "Necessities of Life" clause. His accumulated shipping charges in three years would—

He sucked his breath in sharply. "Smathers?"

"Yes?"

"Listen to me: if I don't buy from the robot, it'll blast me with a Molecular Disruptor. But I *can't* buy from the robot, even if the Company would let me, because I don't have any money. Money's necessary if I want to stay alive. Get it? *Necessary?*"

"No," Smathers said. "I don't get it."

"What I'm saying is that the item I most need to preserve my life is money. It's a *necessity of life*. And therefore you have to supply me gratis with all the money I need, until this robot decides it's sold me enough. If you don't come through, I'll sue the Company for breach of contract."

Smathers grinned. "Try it. You'll be dead before you can contact a lawyer. The robot will kill you."

Sweat poured down Wingert's back, but he felt the moment of triumph approaching. Reaching inside his khaki shirt, he drew out the thick pseudo-parchment sheet that was his contract.

"You refuse! You refuse to supply a necessity of life! The contract," Wingert declared, "is therefore void." Before Smathers' horrified gaze he ripped the document up and tossed the pieces over his shoulder carelessly.

"Having broken your end of the contract," Wingert said, "you relieve me of all further obligations to the Company. Therefore I'll thank you to remove your damned spybeam from my planet."

"*Your* planet?"

"Precisely. Squatter's rights—and since there's no longer

a contract between us, you're forbidden by galactic law to spy on me!"

Smathers looked dazed. "You're a fast talker, Wingert. But we'll fight this. Wait till I refer this upstairs. You won't get out of this so easily!"

Wingert flashed a cocky grin. "Refer it upstairs, if you want. I've got the law on my side."

Smathers snarled and broke the contact.

"Nicely argued," said XL-ad41 approvingly. "I hope you win your case."

"I have to," Wingert said. "They can't touch me, not if their contract is really binding on both parties. If they try to use their spybeam record as evidence against me, it'll show you threatening me. They don't have a leg to stand on."

"But how about me? I—"

"I haven't forgotten. There is a Molecular Disruptor in your belly waiting to disrupt me." Wingert grinned at the robot. "Look here, XL-ad41, face facts: you're a lousy salesman. You have a certain degree of misused guile, but you lack tact, subtlety. You can't go selling people things at gunpoint very long without involving your manufacturers in an interstellar war. As soon as you get back to Densobol and they find out what you've done, they'll dismantle you quicker than you can sell a Dreeg-Skinner."

"I was thinking that myself," the robot admitted.

"Good. But I'll make a suggestion: I'll *teach* you how to be a salesman. I used to be one, myself; besides, I'm an Earthman, and innately shrewd. When I'm through with you, you move on to the next planet—I think your makers will forgive you if you make an extra stop—and sell out all your stock."

"It sounds wonderful," XL-ad41 said.

"One string is attached. In return for the education I'll give you, you're to supply me with such things as I need to live comfortably here on a permanent basis. Cigars, magneboots, short-range transmitters, depilator, etc. I'm sure your manufacturers will think it's a fair exchange, my profitmaking shrewdness for your magneboots. Oh, and I'll need one of those force-field generators too— just in case the Company shows up and tries to make trouble."

The robot glowed happily. "I'm sure such an exchange can be arranged. I believe this now makes us partners."

"It does indeed," Wingert said. "As your first lesson, let me show you an ancient Terran custom that a good salesman ought to know." He gripped the robot's cold metal hand firmly in his own. "Shake, partner!"

ADRIFT ON THE POLICY LEVEL

by CHAN DAVIS

> *Dr. H. Chandler Davis is one man. At Princeton's Institute for Advanced Studies, the doctor delves into more complicated aspects of the higher reaches of mathematics than the rest of us are ever likely to encounter; but inside the body of the mathematician lives another man whose interests are lighter, brighter and well worth the time of any science-fiction reader—for example, this cheerful story of a cheerless future.*

I

J. Albert LaRue was nervous, but you couldn't blame him. It was his big day. He looked up for reassurance at the big, bass-voiced man sitting so stolidly next to him in the hissing subway car, and found what he sought.

There was plenty of reassurance in having a man like Calvin Boersma on your side.

Albert declared mildly but firmly: "One single thought is uppermost in my mind."

Boersma inclined his ear. "What?"

"Oxidase epsilon!" cried Albert.

Cal Boersma clapped him on the shoulder and answered, like a fight manager rushing last-minute strategies to his boxer: "The one single thought that *should* be uppermost in your mind is *selling* oxidase epsilon. Nothing will be done unless The Corporation is sold on it. And when you deal with Corporation executives you're dealing with experts."

LaRue thought that over, swaying to the motion of the car.

"We do have something genuinely important to sell, don't we?" he ventured. He had been studying oxidase epsilon for three years. Boersma, on the other hand, was involved in the matter only because he was LaRue's lab-assistant's brother-in-law, an assistant sales manager of a plastics firm . . . and the only businessman LaRue knew.

Still, today—the big day—Cal Boersma was the expert. The promoter. The man who was right in the thick of the hard, practical world outside the University's cloistered halls—the world that terrified J. Albert LaRue.

Cal was all reassurance. "Oxidase epsilon *is* important, all right. That's the only reason we have a chance."

Their subway car gave a long, loud whoosh, followed by a shrill hissing. They were at their station. J. Albert LaRue felt a twinge of apprehension. This, he told himself, was it! They joined the file of passengers leaving the car for the luxurious escalator.

"Yes, Albert," Cal rumbled, as they rode up side by side, "we have something big here, if we can reach the top men—say, the Regional Director. Why, Albert, this could get you an assistant section managership in The Corporation itself!"

"Oh, thank you! But of course I wouldn't want— I mean, my devotion to research—" Albert was flustered.

"But of course I could take care of that end of it for you," Boersma said reassuringly. "Well, here we are, Albert."

The escalator fed them into a sunlit square between twenty-story buildings. A blindlingly green mall crossed the square to the Regional Executive Building of The Corporation. Albert could not help being awed. It was a truly impressive structure—a block wide, only three stories high.

Cal said, in a reverent growl: "Putting up a building like that in the most heavily taxed area of Detroit—you know what that symbolizes, Albert? *Power.* Power and salesmanship! That's what you're dealing with when you deal with The Corporation."

The building was the hub of the Lakes Region, and the architecture was appropriately monumental. Albert murmured a comment, impressed. Cal agreed. "Superbly styled," he said solemnly.

Glass doors extending the full height of the building opened smoothly at the touch of Albert's hand. Straight ahead across the cool lobby another set of glass doors equally tall, were a showcase for dramatic exhibits of The Corporation's activities. Soothing lights rippled through an enchanged twilight. Glowing letters said, "Museum of Progress."

Several families on holiday wandered delighted among the exhibits, basking in the highest salesmanship the race had produced.

Albert started automatically in that direction. Cal's hand on his arm stopped him. "This way, Albert. The corridor to the right."

"Huh? But—I thought you said you couldn't get an appointment, and we'd have to follow the same channels as any member of the public." Certainly the "public" was the delighted wanderer through those gorgeous glass doors.

"Oh, sure, that's what we're doing. But I didn't mean *that* public."

"Oh." Apparently the Museum was only for the herd. Albert humbly followed Cal (not without a backward glance) to the relatively unobtrusive door at the end of the lobby—the initiate's secret passage to power, he thought with deep reverence.

But he noticed that three or four new people just entering the building were turning the same way.

A waiting room. But it was not a disappointing one; evidently Cal had directed them right; they had passed to a higher circle. The room was large, yet it looked like a sanctum.

Albert had never seen chairs like these. All of the twenty-five or so men and women who were there ahead of them were distinctly better dressed than Albert. On the other hand Cal's suit—a one-piece wooly buff-colored outfit, fashionably loose at the elbows and knees—was a match for any of them. Albert took pride in that.

Albert sat and fidgeted. Cal's bass voice gently reminded him that fidgeting would be fatal, then rehearsed him in his approach. He was to be, basically, a professor of plant metabolism; it was a poor approach, Cal conceded regretfully, but the only one Albert was qualified to make. Salesmanship he was to leave to Cal; his own appeal was to be based on his position—such as it was—as a scientific expert; therefore he was to be, basically, himself. His success in projecting the role might possibly be decisive—although the main responsibility, Cal pointed out, was Cal's.

While Cal talked, Albert fidgeted and watched the room. The lush chairs, irregularly placed, still managed all to face one wall, and in that wall were three plain doors. From time to time an attendant would appear to call one of the waiting supplicants to one of the doors. The attendants were liveried young men with flowing black hair. Finally, one came their way! He summoned them with a bow—an eye-flashing, head-tossing, flourishing bow, like a dancer rather than a butler.

Albert followed Cal to the door. "Will this be a junior executive? A personal secretary? A—"

But Cal seemed not to hear.

Albert followed Cal through the door and saw the most beautiful girl in the world.

He couldn't look at her, not by a long way. She was much too beautiful for that. But he knew exactly what she looked like. He could see in his mind her shining, ringleted hair falling gently to her naked shoulders, her dazzling bright expressionless face. He couldn't even think about her body; it was terrifying.

She sat behind a desk and looked at them.

Cal struck a masterful pose, his arms folded. "We have come on a scientific matter," he said haughtily, "not familiar to The Corporation, concerning several northern colonial areas."

She wrote deliberately on a small plain pad. Tonelessly, sweetly, she asked, "Your name?"

"Calvin Boersma."

Her veiled eyes swung to Albert. He couldn't possibly

speak. His whole consciousness was occupied in not looking at her.

Cal said sonorously: "This is J. Albert LaRue, Professor of Plant Metabolism." Albert was positively proud of his name, the way Cal said it.

The most beautiful girl in the world whispered meltingly: "Go out this door and down the corridor to Mr. Blick's office. He'll be expecting you."

Albert chose this moment to try to look at her. And *she smiled!* Albert, completely routed, rushed to the door. He was grateful she hadn't done *that* before! Cal, with his greater experience and higher position in life, could linger a moment, leaning on the desk, to leer at her.

But all the same, when they reached the corridor, he was sweating.

Albert said carefully, "*She* wasn't an executive, was she?"

"No," said Cal, a little scornfully. "She's an Agency Model, what else? Of course, you probably don't see them much at the University, except at the Corporation Representative's Office and maybe the President's Office." Albert had never been near either. "She doesn't have much to do except to impress visitors, and of course stop the ones that don't belong here."

Albert hesitated. "She *was* impressive."

"She's impressive, all right," Cal agreed. "When you consider the Agency rates, and then realize that any member of the public who comes to the Regional Executive Building on business sees an Agency Model receptionist —then you know you're dealing with power, Albert."

Albert had a sudden idea. He ventured: "Would we have done better to have brought an Agency Model with us?"

Cal stared. "To go through the whole afternoon with us? Impossible, Albert! It'd cost you a year's salary."

Albert said eagerly: "No, that's the beauty of it, Cal! You see, I have a young cousin—I haven't seen her recently, of course, but she was drafted by the Agency, and I might have been able to get her to—" He faltered. Boersma was looking scandalized.

"Albert— excuse me. If your cousin had so much as walked into any business office with makeup on, she'd have had to collect Agency rates—or she'd have been out of the Agency like *that*. And owing them plenty." He finished consolingly, "A Model wouldn't have done the trick anyway."

II

Mr. Blick looked more like a scientist than a businessman, and his desk was a bit of a laboratory. At his left hand was an elaborate switchboard, curved so all parts would be in easy reach; most of the switches were in rows, the handles color-coded. As he nodded Cal to a seat his fingers flicked over three switches. The earphones and microphone clamped on his head had several switches too, and his right hand quivered beside a stenotype machine of unfamiliar complexity.

He spoke in an undertone into his mike, then his hand whizzed almost invisibly over the stenotype.

"Hello, Mr. Boersma," he said, flicking one last switch but not removing the earphones. "Please excuse my idiosyncrasies, it seems I actually work better this way." His voice was firm, resonant and persuasive.

Cal took over again. He opened with a round compliment for Mr. Blick's battery of gadgets, and then flowed smoothly on to an even more glowing series of compliments—which Albert realized with a qualm of embarrassment referred to *him*.

After the first minute or so, though, Albert found the talk less interesting than the interruptions. Mr. Blick would raise a forefinger apologetically but fast; switches would tumble; he would listen to the earphones, whisper into the mike, and perform incredibly on the absolutely silent stenotype. Shifting lights touched his face, and Albert realized the desk top contained at least one TV screen, as well as a bank of blinking colored lights. The moment the interruption was disposed of, Mr. Blick's faultless diction and pleasant voice would return Cal exactly to where he'd been. Albert was impressed.

Cal's peroration was an urgent appeal that Mr. Blick consider the importance to The Corporation, financially, of what he was about to learn. Then he turned to Albert, a little too abruptly.

"One single thought is uppermost in my mind," Albert stuttered, caught off guard. "Oxidase epsilon. I am resolved that The Corporation shall be made to see the importance—"

"Just a moment, Professor LaRue," came Mr. Blick's smooth Corporation voice. "You'll have to explain this to *me*. I don't have the background or the brains that you people in the academic line have. Now in layman's terms, just what *is* oxidase epsilon?" He grinned handsomely.

"Oh, don't feel bad," said Albert hastily. "Lots of my colleagues haven't heard of it, either." This was only a half-truth. Every one of his colleagues that Albert met at the University in a normal working month had certainly heard of oxidase epsilon—from Albert. "It's an enzyme found in many plants but recognized only recently. You see, many of the laboratory species created during the last few decades have been unable to produce ordinary oxidase, or oxidase alpha, but surprisingly enough some of these have survived. This is due to the presence of a series of related compounds, of which oxidases beta, gamma, delta, and epsilon have been isolated, and beta and epsilon have been prepared in the laboratory."

Mr. Blick shifted uncertainly in his seat. Albert hurried on so he would see how simple it all was. "I have been studying the reactions catalyzed by oxidase epsilon in several species of *Triticum*. I found quite unexpectedly that none of them produce the enzyme themselves. Amazing, isn't it? All the oxidase epsilon in those plants comes from a fungus, *Puccinia triticina*, which infects them. This, of course, explains the failure of Hinshaw's group to produce viable *Triticum kacl* following—"

Mr. Blick smiled handsomely again. "Well now, Professor LaRue, you'll have to tell me what this means. In *my* terms—you understand."

Cal boomed portentously, "It may mean the saving of the economies of three of The Corporation's richest colonies." Rather dramatic, Albert thought.

Mr. Blick said appreciatively, "Very good. *Very* good. Tell me more. Which colonies—and why?" His right hand left its crouch to spring restlessly to the stenotype.

Albert resumed, buoyed by this flattering show of interest. "West Lapland in Europe, and Great Slave and Churchill on this continent. They're all Corporation colonies, recently opened up for wheat-growing by *Triticum witti,* and I've been told they're extremely productive."

"Who is Triticum Witti? One of our vice-presidents?"

Albert, shocked, explained patiently, *"Triticum witti* is one of the new species of wheat which depend on oxidase epsilon. And if the fungus *Puccinia triticina* on that wheat becomes a pest, sprays may be used to get rid of it. And a whole year's wheat crop in those colonies may be destroyed."

"Destroyed," Mr. Blick repeated wonderingly. His forefinger silenced Albert like a conductor's baton; then both his hands danced over keys and switches, and he was muttering into his microphone again.

Another interruption, thought Albert. He felt proper reverence for the undoubted importance of whatever Mr. Blick was settling, still he was bothered a little, too. Actually (he remembered suddenly) he had a reason to be so presumptuous: oxidase epsilon was important, too. Over five hundred million dollars had gone into those three colonies already, and no doubt a good many people.

However, it turned out this particular interruption must have been devoted to West Lapland, Great Slave, and Churchill after all. Mr. Blick abandoned his instrument panel and announced his congratulations to them: "Mr. Boersma, the decision has been made to assign an expediter to your case!" And he smiled heartily.

This was a high point for Albert.

He wasn't sure he knew what an expediter was, but he was sure from Mr. Blick's manner that an unparalleled honor had been given him. It almost made him dizzy to think of all this glittering building, all the attendants and Models and executives, bowing to *him,* as Mr. Blick's manner implied they must.

A red light flicked on and off on Mr. Blick's desk. As he turned to it he said, "Excuse me, gentlemen." Of course, Albert pardoned him mentally, you have to work.

He whispered to Cal, "Well, I guess we're doing pretty well."

"Huh? Oh, yes, very well," Cal whispered back. "So far."

"So far? Doesn't Mr. Blick understand the problem? All we have to do is give him the details now."

"Oh, no, Albert! I'm sure *he* can't make the decision. He'll have to send us to someone higher up."

Higher up? "Why? Do we have to explain it all over again?"

Cal turned in his chair so he could whisper to Albert less conspicuously. "Albert, an enterprise the size of The Corporation can't give consideration to every crackpot suggestion anyone tries to sell it. There have to be regular channels. Now the Plant Metabolism Department doesn't have any connections here (maybe we can do something about that), so we have to run a sort of obstacle course. It's survival of the fittest, Albert! Only the most worthwhile survive to see the Regional Director. Of course the Regional Director selects which of those to accept, but he doesn't have to sift through a lot of crackpot propositions."

Albert could see the analogy to natural selection. Still, he asked humbly: "How do you know the best suggestions get through? Doesn't it depend a lot on how good a salesman is handling them?"

"Very much so. Naturally!"

"But then— Suppose, for instance, I hadn't happened to know you. My good idea wouldn't have got past Mr. Blick."

"It wouldn't have got past the Model," Cal corrected. "Maybe not that far. But you see in that case it wouldn't have been a very important idea, because it wouldn't have been *put into effect*." He said it with a very firm, practical jawline. "Unless of course someone else had had the initiative and resourcefulness to present the same idea better. Do you see now? *Really important ideas attract the sales talent to put them across.*"

Albert didn't understand the reasoning, he had to admit. It was such an important point, and he was missing it. He reminded himself humbly that a scientist is no expert outside his own field.

So all Mr. Blick had been telling them was that they had not yet been turned down. Albert's disappointment was sharp.

Still, he was curious. How had such a trivial announcement given him such euphoria? Could you produce that kind of effect just by your delivery? Mr. Blick could, apparently. The architecture, the Model, and all the rest had been build-up for him; and certainly they had helped the effect; but they didn't explain it.

What was the key? *Personality,* Albert realized. This was what businessmen meant by their technical term "personality". Personality was the asset Mr. Blick had exploited to rise to where he was—rather than becoming, say, a scientist.

The Blicks and Boersmas worked hard at it. Wistfully, Albert wondered how it was done. Of course the experts in this field didn't publish their results, and anyhow he had never studied it. But it was the most important field of human culture, for on it hinged the policy decisions of government—even of The Corporation!

He couldn't estimate whether Cal was as good as Mr. Blick, because he assumed Cal had never put forth a big effort on him, Albert. He wasn't worth it.

He had one other question for Cal. "What is an expediter?"

"Oh, I thought you knew," boomed Cal. "They can be a big help. That's why we're doing well to be assigned one. We're going to get into the *top levels,* Albert, where only a salesman of true merit can hope to put across an idea. An expediter can do it if anyone can. The expediters are too young to hold Key Executive Positions, but they're Men On The Way Up. They—"

Mr. Blick turned his head toward a door on his left, putting the force of his personality behind the gesture. "Mr. Demarest," he announced as the expediter walked into the room.

III

Mr. Demarest had captivating red curly sideburns, striking brown eyes, and a one-piece coverall in a somewhat loud pattern of black and beige. He almost trembled with excess energy. It was contagious; it made you feel as if you were as abnormally fit as he was.

He grinned his welcome at Albert and Cal, and chuckled merrily: "How do you do, Mr. Boersma."

It was as if Mr. Blick had been turned off. Albert hardly knew he was still in the room. Clearly Mr. Demarest was a Man On The Way Up indeed.

They rose and left the room with him—to a new corridor, very different from the last: weirdly lighted from a strip two feet above the floor, and lined with abstract statuary.

This, together with Mr. Demarest, made a formidable challenge.

Albert rose to it recklessly. "Oxidase epsilon," he proclaimed, "may mean the saving of three of The Corporation's richest colonies!"

Mr. Demarest responded with enthusiasm. "I agree one hundred percent—our Corporation's crop of *Triticum witti* must be saved! Mr. Blick sent me a playback of your explanation by interoffice tube, Professor LaRue. You've got me on your side one hundred per cent! I want to assure you both, very sincerely, that I'll do my utmost to sell Mr. Southfield. Professor, you be ready to fill in the details when I'm through with what I know."

There was no slightest condescension or reservation in his voice. He would take care of things, Albert knew. What a relief!

Cal came booming in: "Your Mr. Blick seems like a competent man."

What a way to talk about a Corporation executive! Albert decided it was not just a simple faux pas, though. Apparently Cal had decided he had to be accepted by Mr. Demarest as an equal, and this was his opening. It seemed risky to Albert. In fact, it frightened him.

"There's just one thing, now, about your Mr. Blick," Cal was saying to Mr. Demarest, with a tiny wink that Albert was proud of having spotted. "I couldn't help wondering how he manages to find so much to do with those switches of his." Albert barely restrained a groan.

But Mr. Demarest grinned! "Frankly, Cal," he answered, "I'm not just sure how many of old Blick's switches are dummies."

Cal had succeeded! That was the main content of Mr. Demarest's remark.

But *were* Mr. Blick's switches dummies? Things were much simpler back—way back—at the University, where people said what they meant.

They were near the end of the corridor. Mr. Demarest said softly, "Mr. Southfield's Office." Clearly Mr. Southfield's presence was enough to curb even Mr. Demarest's boyishness.

They turned through an archway into a large room, lighted like the corridor, with statuary wilder still.

Mr. Southfield was at one side, studying papers in a vast easy chair: an elderly man, fantastically dressed but with a surprisingly ordinary face peeping over the crystal ruff on his magenta leotards. He ignored them. Mr. Demarest made it clear they were supposed to wait until they were called on.

Cal and Albert chose two of the bed-sized chairs facing Mr. Southfield, and waited expectantly.

Mr. Demarest whispered, "I'll be back in time to make the first presentation. Last-minute brush-up, you know." He grinned and clapped Cal smartly on the shoulder. Albert was relieved that he didn't do the same to him, but just shook his hand before leaving. It would have been too upsetting.

Albert sank back in his chair, tired from all he'd been through and relaxed by the soft lights.

It was the most comfortable chair he'd ever been in. It was more than comfortable, it was a deliciously irresistible invitation to relax completely. Albert was barely awake enough to notice that the chair was rocking him gently, tenderly massaging his neck and back.

He lay there, ecstatic. He didn't quite go to sleep. If the chair had been designed just a little differently, no doubt, it could have put him to sleep, but this one just let him rest carefree and mindless.

Cal spoke (and even Cal's quiet bass sounded harsh and urgent): "Sit up straighter, Albert!"

"Why?"

"Albert, any sales resistance you started with is going to be completely *gone* if you don't sit up enought to shut off that chair!"

"Sales resistance?" Albert pondered comfortably. "What have we got to worry about? Mr. Demarest is on our side, isn't he?"

"Mr. Demarest," Cal pointed out, "is *not* the Regional Director."

So they still might have problems! So the marvelous chair was just another trap where the unfit got lost! Albert resolved to himself: "From now on, one single thought will be uppermost in my mind: defending my sales resistance."

He repeated this to himself.

He repeated it again. . . .

"Albert!" There was genuine panic in Cal's voice now.

A fine way to defend his sales resistance! He had let the chair get him again. Regretfully he shifted his weight forward, reaching for the arms of the chair.

"*Watch it!*" said Cal. "Okay now, but don't use the arms. Just lean yourself forward. There." He explained, "The surface on the arms is rough and moist, and I can't think of any reason it should be—unless it's to give you narcotic through the skin! Tiny amounts, of course. But we can't afford any. First time I've ever seen that one in actual use," he admitted.

Albert was astonished, and in a moment he was more so. "Mr. Southfield's chair is the same as ours, and *he's* leaning back in it. Why, he's even stroking the arm while he reads!"

"I know." Cal shook his head. "Remarkable man, isn't he? Remarkable. Remember this, Albert. The true salesman, the man on the very pinnacle of achievement, is also—a connoisseur. Mr. Southfield is a connoisseur. He wants to be presented with the most powerful appeals known, for the sake of the pleasure he gets from the appeal itself. Albert, there is a strong strain of the sensuous, the self-indulgent, in every really successful man like Mr. Southfield. Why? Because to be successful he must have the most profound understanding of self-indulgence."

Albert noticed in passing that, just the same, Cal wasn't self-indulgent enough to trust himself to that chair. He didn't even make a show of doing so. Clearly in Mr. Southfield they had met somebody far above Cal's level. It was unnerving. Oxidase epsilon seemed a terribly feeble straw to outweigh such a disadvantage.

Cal went on, "This is another reason for the institution of expediters. The top executive can't work surrounded by inferior salesmanship. He needs the stimulus and the luxury of receiving his data well packaged. The expediters can do it." He leaned over confidentially. "I've heard them called backscratchers for that reason," he whispered.

Albert was flattered that Cal admitted him to this trade joke.

Mr. Southfield looked up at the archway as someone came in—not Mr. Demarest, but a black-haired young woman. Albert looked inquiringly at Cal.

"Just a minute. I'll soon know who she is."

She stood facing Mr. Southfield, against the wall opposite Albert and Cal. Mr. Southfield said in a drowsy half-whisper, "Yes, Miss Drury, the ore-distribution pattern. Go on."

"She must be another expediter, on some other matter," Cal decided. "Watch her work, Albert. You won't get an opportunity like this often."

Albert studied her. She was not at all like an Agency Model; she was older than most of them (about thirty); she was fully dressed, in a rather sober black and gray business suit, snug around the hips; and she wasn't wearing makeup. She couldn't be even an ex-Model, she wasn't the type. Heavier in build, for one thing, and though she was very pretty it wasn't that unhuman blinding beauty. On the contrary, Albert enjoyed looking at her (even lacking Mr. Southfield's connoisseurship). He found Miss Drury's warm dark eyes and confident posture very pleasant and relaxing.

She began to talk, gently and musically, something about how to compute the most efficient routing of metallic ore traffic in the Great Lakes Region. Her voice became a chant, rising and falling, but with a little catch in it now and then. Lovely!

Her main device, though, sort of snuck up on him, the way the chair had. It had been going on for some time before Albert was conscious of it. It was like the chair.

Miss Drury moved.

Her hips swung. Only a centimeter each way, but very, very sensuously. You could follow the motion in detail, because her dress was more than merely snug around the hips, you could see every muscle on her belly. The motion seemed entirely spontaneous, but Albert knew she must have worked hard on it.

The knowledge, however, didn't spoil his enjoyment.

"Gee," he marveled to Cal, "how can Mr. Southfield hear what she's saying?"

"Huh? Oh—she lowers her voice from time to time on

purpose so we won't overhear Corporation secrets, but he's much nearer her than we are."

"That's not what I mean!"

"You mean why doesn't her delivery distract him from the message? Albert," Boersma said wisely, "if you were sitting in his chair you'd be getting the message, too—with crushing force. A superior presentation *always* directs attention to the message. But in Mr. Southfield's case it actually stimulates critical consideration as well! Remarkable man. An expert and a connoisseur."

Meanwhile Albert saw that Miss Drury had finished. Maybe she would stay and discuss her report with Mr. Southfield? No, after just a few words he dismissed her.

IV

In a few minutes the glow caused by Miss Drury had changed to a glow of excited pride.

Here was he, plain old Professor LaRue, witnessing the drama of the nerve center of the Lakes Region—the interplay of titanic personalities, deciding the fate of millions. Why, he was even going to be involved in one of the decisions! He hoped the next expediter to see Mr. Southfield would be Mr. Demarest!

Something bothered him. "Cal, how can Mr. Demarest possibly be as—well—persuasive as Miss Drury? I mean—"

"Now, Albert, you leave that to him. Sex is not the only possible vehicle. Experts can make strong appeals to the weakest and subtlest of human drives— even altruism! Oh yes, I know it's surprising to the layman, but even altruism can be useful."

"Really?" Albert was grateful for every tidbit.

"Real masters will sometimes prefer such a method out of sheer virtuosity," whispered Cal.

Mr. Southfield stirred a little in his chair, and Albert snapped to total alertness.

Sure enough, it was Mr. Demarest who came through the archway.

Certainly his entrance was no let down. He strode in even more eagerly than he had into Mr. Blick's office. His costume glittered, his brown eyes glowed. He stood against the wall beyond Mr. Southfield; not quite straight, but with a slight wrestler's crouch. A taut spring.

He gave Albert and Cal only half a second's glance, but that glance was a tingling communication of comradeship and joy of battle. Albert felt himself a participant in something heroic.

Mr. Demarest began releasing all that energy slowly. He gave the background of West Lapland, Great Slave, and Churchill. Maps were flashed on the wall beside him (exactly how, Albert didn't follow), and the drama of arctic colonization was recreated by Mr. Demarest's sportscaster's voice. Albert would have thought Mr. Demarest was the overmodest hero of each project if he hadn't known all three had been done simultaneously. No, it was hard to believe, but all these vivid facts must have been served to Mr. Demarest by some research flunky within the last few minutes. And yet, how he had transfigured them!

The stirring narrative was reaching Mr. Southfield, too. He had actually sat up out of the easy chair.

Mr. Demarest's voice, like Miss Drury's, dropped in volume now and then. Albert and Cal were just a few feet too far away to overhear Corporation secrets.

As the saga advanced, Mr. Demarest changed from Viking to Roman. His voice, by beautifully controlled stages, became bubbling and hedonistic. Now, he was talking about grandiose planned expansions—and, best of all, about how much money The Corporation expected to make from the three colonies. The figures drooled through loose lips. He clapped Mr. Southfield on the shoulder. He stroked Mr. Southfield's arm; when he came to the estimated trade balances, he tickled his neck. Mr. Southfield showed his appreciation of the change in mood by lying back in his chair again.

This didn't stop Mr. Demarest.

It seemed almost obscene. Albert covered his embarrassment by whispering, "I see why they call them backscratchers."

Cal frowned, waved him silent, and went on watching.

Suddenly Mr. Demarest's tone changed again: it became bleak, bitter, desperate. A threat to the calculated return on The Corporation's investment—even to the capital investment itself!

Mr. Southfield sat forward attentively to hear about this danger. Was that good? He hadn't done that with Miss Drury.

What Mr. Demarest said about the danger was, of course, essentially what Albert had told Mr. Blick, but Albert realized that it sounded a lot more frightening Mr. Demarest's way. When he was through, Albert felt physically chilly. Mr. Southfield sat saying nothing. What was he thinking? Could he fail to see the tragedy that threatened?

After a moment he nodded and said, "Nice presentation." He hadn't said that to Miss Drury, Albert exulted!

Mr. Demarest looked dedicated.

Mr. Southfield turned his whole body to face Albert, and looked him straight in the eyes. Albert was too alarmed to look away. Mr. Southfield's formerly ordinary jaw now jutted, his chest swelled imposingly. *"You,* I understand, are a well-informed worker on plant metabolism."* His voice seemed to grow too, until it rolled in on Albert from all sides of the room. "Is it *your* opinion that the danger is great enough to justify taking up the time of the Regional Director?"

It wasn't fair. Mr. Southfield against J. Albert LaRue was a ridiculous mismatch anyway! And now Albert was taken by surprise—after too long a stretch as an inactive spectator—and hit with the suggestion that he had been *wasting Mr. Southfield's time* . . . that his proposition was not only not worth acting on, it was *a waste of the Regional Director's time.*

Albert struggled to speak.

Surely, after praising Mr. Demarest's presentation, Mr. Southfield would be lenient; he would take into account Albert's limited background; he wouldn't expect too much. Albert struggled to say anything.

He couldn't open his mouth.

As he sat staring at Mr. Southfield, he could feel his own shoulders drawing inward and all his muscles going limp.

Cal said, in almost a normal voice, "Yes."

That was enough, just barely. Albert whispered, "Yes," terrified at having found the courage.

Mr. Southfield glared down at him a moment more.

Then he said, "Very well, you may see the Regional Director. Mr. Demarest, take them there."

Albert followed Mr. Demarest blindly. His entire attention was concentrated on recovering from Mr. Southfield.

He had been one up, thanks to Mr. Demarest. Now, how could he have stayed one up? How should he have resisted Mr. Southfield's dizzying display of personality?

He played the episode back mentally over and over, trying to correct it to run as it should have. Finally he succeeded, at least in his mind. He saw what his attitude *should* have been. He *should* have kept his shoulders squared and his vocal cords loose, and faced Mr. Southfield confidently. Now he saw how to do it.

He walked erectly and firmly behind Mr. Demarest, and allowed a haughty half-smile to play on his lips.

He felt armed to face Mr. Southfield all by himself— or, since it seemed Mr. Southfield was not the Regional Director after all, even to face the Regional Director!

They stopped in front of a large double door guarded by an absolutely motionless man with a gun.

"Men," said Mr. Demarest with cheerful innocence, "I wish you luck. I wish you all the luck in the world."

Cal looked suddenly stricken but said, with casualness that didn't fool even Albert, "Wouldn't you like to come in with us?"

"Oh, no. Mr. Southfield told me only to bring you here. I'd be overstepping my bounds if I did any more. But all the good luck in the world, men!"

Cal said hearty goodbyes. But when he turned back to Albert he said, Despairing: "The brushoff."

Albert could hardly take it in. "But— we get to make our presentation to the Regional Director, don't we?"

Boersma shrugged hopelessly, "Don't you see, Albert? Our presentation won't be good enough, without Demarest. When Mr. Southfield sent us on alone he was giving us the brushoff."

"Cal—are *you* going to back out too?"

"I should say not! It's a feather in our cap to have got this far, Albert. We have to follow up just as far as our abilities will take us!"

Albert went to the double door. He worried about the

armed guard for a moment, but they weren't challenged. The guard hadn't even blinked, in fact.

Albert asked Cal, "Then we do still have a chance?"

"No, we haven't got a chance."

He started to push the door open, then hesitated again. "But you'll do your best?"

"I should say so! You don't get to present a proposition to the Regional Director *every* day."

With determination, Albert drew himself even straighter, and prepared himself to meet an onslaught twice as overbearing as Mr. Southfield's. One single thought was uppermost in his mind: defending his sales resistance. He felt inches taller than before; he even slightly looked down at Cal and his pessimism.

Cal pushed the door open and they went in.

The Regional Director sat alone in a straight chair, at a plain desk in a very plain office about the size of most offices.

The Regional Director was a woman.

She was dressed about as any businesswoman might dress; as conservatively as Miss Drury. As a matter of fact, she looked like Miss Drury, fifteen years older. Certainly she had the same black hair and gentle oval face.

What a surprise! A *pleasant* surprise. Albert felt still bigger and more confident than he had outside. He would certainly get on well with this motherly, unthreatening person!

She was reading from a small microfilm viewer on an otherwise bare desk. Obviously she had only a little to do before she would be free. Albert patiently watched her read. She read very conscientiously, that was clear.

After a moment she glanced up at them briefly, with an apologetic smile, then down again. Her shy dark eyes showed so much! You could see how sincerely she welcomed them, and how sorry she was that she had so much work to do—how much she would prefer to be talking with *them*. Albert pitied her. From the bottom of his heart, he pitied her. Why, that small microfilm viewer, he realized, could perfectly well contain volumes of complicated Corporation reports. Poor woman! The poor woman who happened to be Regional Director read on.

Once in a while she passed one hand, wearily but determinedly, across her face. There was a slight droop to her shoulders. Albert pitied her more all the time. She was not too strong—she had such a big job—and she was so courageously trying to do her best with all those reports in the viewer!

Finally she raised her head.

It was clear she was not through; there was no relief on her face. But she raised her head to them.

Her affection covered them like a warm bath. Albert realized he was in a position to do the kindest thing he had ever done. He felt growing in himself the resolution to do it. He would!

He started toward the door.

Before he left she met his eyes once more, and her smile showed *such* appreciation for his understanding!

Albert felt there could be no greater reward.

Out in the park again he realized for the first time that Cal was right behind him.

They looked at each other for a long time.

Then Cal started walking again, toward the subway. "The brushoff," he said.

"I thought you said you'd do your best," said Albert. But he knew that Cal's "I did" was the truth.

They walked on slowly. Cal said, "Remarkable woman. . . . A real master. Sheer virtuosity!"

Albert said, "Our society certainly rewards its most deserving members."

That one single thought was uppermost in his mind, all the long way home.

SPARKIE'S FALL

by GAVIN HYDE

Readers of the (very) short-lived STAR SCIENCE
FICTION MAGAZINE *will remember a tender and
delicate story of a boy and a chess-playing brain,*
NOR THE MOON BY NIGHT. *That was Gavin Hyde's
first story; here is his second; as different from the
first as night from day, and showing a versatility, as
well as a talent, that makes us eagerly await numbers three to infinity.*

Sparkson was relieved to see the evening sky melt into
the terrain of the planet where he had been forced down,
slowly obliterating the forms of the aliens on each side
of him. He had been looking forward to night because
he had thought it over and he hoped—rather optimis-
tically, he admitted to himself—that they might let him
leave the rocket, or something.

Anything.

Anything was better than walking around the ship for
the equivalent of three earth days, the only diversion
being the mechanical Translator and that exasperating as
hell as it tried to make sense of what the alien said and
type it out for him on white little slips of paper: "NAME,
I am worried. Could Sparkie (eat) (be nourished by)
GARBLE?"

And then the answer: "!, (stop) (cease) (desist from)
worrying, NAME. Sparkie is (in admirable condition)
(fine)!"

It had taken him twenty years to get "Sparkie" out of his family's vocabulary. And now the first two "people" he met in outer space called him Sparkie.

Just because they were bigger than he was!

They lay on each side of him, gigantic whales from an ocean of soot, their lights glowing handfuls of sand. Nothing came out, nothing went in.

There were just two.

Many of his controls had ceased to function when they had pulled him down between them. Others were as usual. He couldn't take off, of course—except when that message came out of the Translator: "NAME, Sparkie might (desire) (want) (thirst for) exercise."

He leapt to the chance—it was foolish of them to think that the ship was the man and needed exercise, but that foolishness might help him escape—but they had gone with him, limiting him to graceful figure eights. He tried turning out of one of them, away into space.

He was returned to his place, gently.

When they had captured him, naturally, his first move was to open communications with them through the radio. They received him well, with the help of the translator. They said hello, yes we know where you came from, hope you had a good trip, and then they were quiet.

He had asked them the first forty-nine questions on the checklist designed for making contact with aliens. Nothing. At the end he was yelling at them.

Silence.

Then he forgot his briefings. "What's the matter, battery gone dead?"

They said only: "Time to rest, Sparkie."

They were not exactly their last words, because while he was "exercising" he had asked if he could fire a nuclear missile, hoping to arouse a little more respect.

Then the one that always seemed subservient to the other said, "NAME, I am frightened. Sparkie might not (throw) (hurl) (eject) it free of his vessel. (Moreover) (Also) it might GARBLE the alignment of the GARBLE GARBLE."

The other didn't even answer that. "Fire away, Sparkie!"

So he threw the lever and there was a wondrous sun and a mushroom that would have turned Einstein over in his grave, certainly, if it had grown under him.

One said, "That's (enough) (sufficient) for (period of time)!" And the other said, "Better than 4th of July, eh, Sparkie?"

"It sure is. How come you know about the 4th?"

"We know what we need to know. Let us rest now."

Sparkson tried everything, even "I'm lonely!" But rest it was.

He had slept, getting up to check gauges and read some incredibly garbled messages—conversations having nothing to do with him, that the Translator apparently couldn't begin to handle.

Now, with the coming of night, he stayed by the Translator. After an hour of darkness a short slip of paper appeared.

"Goodnight, NAME."

Then another. "(Sweet) (Pleasant) (Gentle) dreams of mother, NAME."

They were going to sleep. He sat sweating, staring at the slot, with his hands on each side of the gold-braided uniform cap on his head.

After a while some papers slid out of the Translator. Drowsily the aliens were communicating, like girls whispering secret, in bed.

"NAME—"

"?"

"It is (odd) (strange) (perplexing)."

"?"

"I am thinking of Sparkie's mind . . . NAME!"

"I am awake!"

"Sparkie is so (small) (weak) (defenseless)."

"(Hm) (Mm) (Mmm)."

"His mind is like a (piece) (sheet) of GARBLE. We think on the (bases) (conditions) (roots) of our experience, our perceptions which are multiplied by (objects) (things) (forms of matter) which we have sensed. Sparkie must think with the (toys) (playthings) of his earth only. How can he understand us? What does he know of GARBLE, GARBLE or GARBLE for example, this (small) (weak) (defenseless) being? NAME!"

"! Go to sleep."

That was all. He waited another hour. Then he read

the bits of paper, in order. He read them over and over again, while the starless biblical darkness, one thing by God that was not among the *forms of matter,* offered him freedom.

So he was "(small) (weak) (defenseless)"?

He would show them.

He reviewed the gravity and atmospheric tables beside the suit, strapped nuclearms on each side, brought it closed around his body.

As he staggered, arms up and legs bent under the weight, he was made suddenly angry by an insistent tension at the back of his throat.

The "(toys) (playthings)" of his earth indeed!

He opened the hatch.

He jumped to the surface of the. . . . the. . . .

Planet?

This?

Some hours later the Translator in the cold metal hum of the ship began to spit papers, violently.

Waves of magnetism, pulses of electric desire, like startled schools of fish in coral, swept the corridors.

A great rocking bellowing sound and a smell of sorrow spread skyward.

STAR DESCENDING

by ALGIS BUDRYS

> Mr. Budrys asks us to make clear that the title of
> this story is the editor's, not his own. It may be that
> there's a connotation that doesn't belong; but the
> facts are clear. In publishing a fine new story by the
> author of MAN OF EARTH and scores of other
> stories, short and long, STAR does not stoop. It
> beams with pride.

Inconspicuous in his half of the room, which was dark,
Henry Walters watched his partner fraying down into
tatters like a mooring line caught between hull and dock.

It was disquieting to see. Even if you ignored its con-
crete significance—if you ignored the fact that Stephenson might be fighting for Spot Dialogue's life—then
Stephenson became a symbol of all men at tenuous grips
with all frustration. Henry Walters puffed nervously at
his cigarette. His teeth were being set on edge.

In the lighted half of the room, Stephenson, standing
beside Carmer's chair, was starting at the beginning,
again. Like all men at grips with all frustration, he had
begun to abandon politeness as an obstructive luxury.

"What is your name?" Stephenson asked Carmer.

"Carmer." He answered in a husky whisper.

Stephenson nodded. "That's right. That's good. Where
were you this afternoon?" He sounded more like a police
interrogator than a man addressing a client.

"At the corner of Fifth Avenue and Fourteenth Street."

"Yes! That's *good*, Mr. Carmer. Now—what were you doing?"

Henry Walters reflected that Stephenson was showing altogether too much eager expectation. They'd gotten this far a dozen times. Steve, of course, tended to unfounded optimism.

His own stomach muscles tightened, and he leaned forward to catch Carmer's answer.

Carmer shook his head in despair. "I don't know. Again, I don't know."

"But you *do* know, Mr. Carmer! You met a man named Dugan! You—"

Henry Walters had already smashed out his cigarette and passed a hand over the lighting controls. He stood up and interrupted Steve's exasperation.

"Mr. Carmer . . ." The lights came up around him. He shot Stephenson one disgusted look before Carmer had turned his head in response to the interjection. "Mr. Carmer, please accept our sincere apologies for your trouble. We'd like to try one thing more. Would you mind looking at a photographic record of your actions this afternoon?" He ignored Steve's consternation. Getting this settled was more important that Carmer's finding out that Spot Dialogue had eyes as well as ears.

Carmer fumbled at his wilting collar, leaving finger marks when he took his hand away to run it through his tousled hair. Henry Walters reflected that hc'd be leaving fresh marks whcn he next fussed with the collar. But that hardly mattered.

"No," Carmer said. "Uh—*yes*—uh, I mean, no—I would not mind." Carmer's personality, as well as Stephen's, was sacrificing certain luxuries. In the effort to remember where its afternoon had gone, his mind was foregoing the ability to specify and stipulate.

The look Henry Walters gave Stephenson was dark with anger.

This whole interview had been against his better judgment. But they were in it, now—it might as well be done wholehog. He touched a desk switch. One end of the room became a stereographic stage.

It was the corner of Fourteenth Street and Fifth Avenue. Carmer was at the empty taxi stand in front of the Fifth Avenue entrance to the Raymond Building. A cab pulled up, and, as Carmer started for it, a passenger he hadn't noticed straightened up from his slouch in the back seat, paid the driver, and got out. Recognition flickered over Carmer's face, together with a relieved smile.

The other man turned around, saw and recognized Carmer, and stepped forward, holding out his hand.

"Well, hello there," he said.

"Hello, Mr. Dugan," Carmer replied. "I was just on my way home. Didn't think I'd make it to your office in time, so I thought I'd see you tomorrow." He shook his head at the cabby's inquiring look, and the taxi pulled up to the head of the stand and parked, leaving the two of them on the corner.

Dugan smiled. "Small world. I came down to meet my wife. She's doing some shopping, but I'm early. Let's have a drink. Might do some business now. Never put off 'til tomorrow."

"All ri—" Carmer began.

The sound cut off first. A second later, the scene dissolved into a corruscating whirlpool that agonized their eyes for a moment before Henry Walters thumbed the switch and the room lights came back on.

He sighed under his breath and looked inquiringly at Carmer.

The perspiring man hunched in his chair. He shook his head dully. "I'm sorry," he said helplessly, "but I can't remember past that point. I don't know what happened afterward."

Henry Walters' tongue clicked away from his palate in a small sound of finality.

"Thank you, Mr. Carmer. "We're deeply appreciative of your cooperation. I'm only sorry you couldn't clear up the difficulty. We retained the services of an excellent psychiatrist, for use in the event that our own efforts were unsuccessful. He is available for immediate session, if you wish. There is no charge, of course, and we're refunding your fee. Thank you again for your willingness to help us. And please be assured that we will not be satisfied until we have made full amends to you."

It didn't much matter what he said, specifically, as long as he extended both apologies and further help. Carmer was still pretty much in shock—had been, ever since Spot Dialogue's emergency squad had brought him back from the corner where he'd been wandering aimlessly.

"Psychiatrist, huh?" he muttered under his breath. "Yeah. Yes—good idea."

Henry Walters picked up an office phone and called a staff member to come take Carmer down to the psychiatrist. While they waited, he looked coldly at Stephenson, who was uncomfortably trying to retain his slipping hold on a neutral facial expression.

Henry Walters waited until Carmer had left the room. He held Stephenson in the vise of his look, and his look grew tighter and tighter.

Stephenson screamed for mercy, in his own characteristic way.

He mopped his face and tried to explain. "Look, Henry —I still say it made sense to try it my way. Carmer was amnesiac, sure, but there was a good chance he'd snap out of it with a little prodding. Now what's going to happen? We send him to a psychiatrist. Okay. The headshrinker fixes him up. Then what does Carmer do? He goes home and tells his friends Spot Dialogue fouled him up so badly that he had to be bailed out of it with psychiatric treatment."

He gestured helplessly and slapped his fist in agony. "Inside of a week, we won't have a client left!" He looked back at Henry Walters in puzzlement, wondering why he had not been interrupted.

Henry Walters raised a finger. "One:" he said, "Carmer subscribed to Spot Dialogue because he doesn't think he can meet the competition by himself. The essence of Spot Dialogue's service is that we provide each man with an instantaneous research and counseling service that's guaranteed to pull him out of any tough spot. He doesn't know how we do it, and he isn't specially concerned. He knows we watch over him, and, whether it's swinging a business deal or making time with a cute little thing from Four Oaks, Ohio, we'll see him through.

"Two: it follows that Carmer is unconsciously convinced of his inability to do the right thing. I'm not interested in the conditioning, childhood environment, heredity, or any other mental cat's-cradle that led him to that conclusion. All I know is that he *was* led to it. He wouldn't be a subscriber if he hadn't.

"Three: it follows that Carmer will feel that the fault is somehow in himself, not in Spot Dialogue. He will *not* tell his friends we failed him. Being convinced that he failed himself, he will not tell his friends *anything*."

"Four: by dragging him up here and trying shotgun methods on him, you came close to spilling the beans. He was very close to realizing that we're just as scared—more so—than he is. Steve, you're my partner because you have the business front and I don't. But I'm your partner because I set up this outfit, and I've got the brains and you have not. So, if you don't mind, I'll do the thinking while you stick to popularizing my product."

Stephenson flushed a meaty red. He opened his mouth.

"Five:" Henry Walters said, "You know I'm right. More important, I know I'm right."

Stephenson let his mouth close. He took a deep breath. "Well," he said finally, "Well—so we *are* in the clear. Carmer won't talk. That takes care of that," he added with relief.

Henry Walters shook his head with the cold inexorability of a computing robot. "We are *not*. Our pickups went haywire at the exact same instant as Cramer went amnesiac."

Stephenson shrugged. "Coincidental equipment failure."

Henry Walters pursed his lips as though to spit. "Item: Spot Dialogue does not have equipment failures. In terms of the field mechanics, it's impossible. Item: Carmer does not have amnesia. If he can remember Dugan at all, the trouble's not connected with anything he and Dugan might have said or done to each other. He was not—" this was said with heavy scorn—"hit on the head by a falling object, *a la* popular fiction. We are not actors in a psychological drama. Carmer was heterodyned, pure and simple, at the same time and by the same means, as our equipment was. Conclusion: someone else has learned how to set up a hyperspatial field, and deliberately threw a monkey wrench into us. Why? Because our particular bowl of gravy has attracted its first fly. Yes, Steve, conservatively speaking, we are in trouble."

That was Monday, and Carmer had been under the routine supervision of a Constant Service operator. On

Tuesday, handling a Special, Henry Walters had the next one happen to him.

The client's name was Dietz.

Spot Dialogue had contracted to see him through one specific situation. Henry Walters was on it because Dietz's account would be highly valuable, if he could be convinced of Spot Dialogue's effectiveness.

Specials were fairly easy. Since the client could brief them on what was coming, SD's research staff was able to compile pertinent data ahead of time. There was only a low expectation of sudden calls on the research division, and, with time to familiarize himself, the operator could do an even smoother job than usual.

Grinning with a faint trace of contempt—as he did every time he sat behind a pickup console—Henry Walters settled himself in his operator's chair, energized the pickup, and waited, his head encased in the opaque fishbowl of the pickup receptor. The earpieces rested snugly against his skull, cutting off all sound from the room. His cheeks were pressed by the rubber padding of the lenses over his eyes.

The search signal rippled through hyperspace, found Dietz, and keyed in the receptors. The carrier wave built up, and Henry Walters looked at Dietz from all around him. He reached out to the console, selected his viewpoint angle, and found himself looking Dietz in the face. He touched the selector again, and saw what Dietz was looking at. He turned the sound on and listened.

Dietz was talking to a secretary in the front office of the man he'd come to see. Dietz's eyes were taking almost criminal advantage of her.

"Will you take a seat, please?" she said, smiling.

Henry Walters touched the research connection. The auxiliary signal dropped into the timelessness of hyperspace, where Research had set up its bubble. "Testing," he said.

The staff member on the other end acknowledged. "Clear," he said.

"Ready on the Dietz job."

"Dietz, okay. We're hooked in."

The complete network was established. If anything unexpected developed, Research would cut in on the circuit, play back its recording of Dietz's activities, consult, and give Henry Walters the information. He, in turn, would whisper the proper move in Dietz's ear. The process was, of course, instantaneous.

"Certainly," Dietz replied. He crossed to a lounge chair and sat down. Henry Walters waited until his eyes were momentarily away from the girl before he pushed the IN button on the console.

The crooked grin intensified. The IN button activated the speaker inside the client's ear. The client naturally assumed the pickup began simultaneously—if he went to the trouble of assuming a pickup at all. Who can divine the ways of omniscience?

Dietz acknowledged his awareness of the pickup with a short, sharp nod—and thereafter kept his eyes away from the secretary. He could not be sure, of course, that Spot Dialogue was watching—but why take chances?

Henry Walters almost chuckled.

"You may go in now," the secretary said.

"Thank you," Dietz answered. He stood up and went to the door of the inner office, which was opened for him by Wilke, the man he'd come to see.

Wilke looked directly into Dietz's eyes, and, past them, into Henry Walters'.

"Tough luck, Mr. Walters," he said, and the pickup seemed to go to pieces around Henry Walters' head.

Stephenson handed him the aspirin with trembling fingers. The glass of water had slopped over and wet his hand.

Henry Walters groped out, swallowed the tablets, and gulped the water. He rubbed his eyes heavily.

"How frightened are you, Steve?" he asked, despite the fact that the pain was burrowing in terror through his brain.

"I don't know, Henry," Stephenson said in a small voice. "I don't think I'd better let myself know."

Henry Walters chuckled crookedly. "The devil we know is a terrible devil indeed, eh? Well, now we know how the clients feel—except that the clients know that whatever watches over them is on their side."

"Henry!"

"Don't exert yourself, Steve. We have no more secrets, and I'm quite sure our opponents *want* us to be aware of them. Whether I acknowledge my awareness now or at some guarded midnight meeting, they'll know I know. Accustom yourself to living with no privacy, Steve—if you can."

"What about you?"

Henry Walters laughed. "What a man does, and says, is never as significant or important as what he thinks. And plans." He looked into thin air and said "I'd keep that mind," to his opponent's listening operator.

"Steve," he went on, "they can't beat me. And if they'll think a moment, they'll see why. I invented the mechanics of this. I set up the organization that is Spot Dialogue. I recruited you, Steve, to make the contacts and do the selling. You make an excellent salesman for a mystical product—omniscience—because even you regard it as a mystical product. It is not. It is good, hard, practical stuff. I'm intelligent, yes. More intelligent, almost certainly, than any of our customers. But *I* don't know *everything*. I don't have to. I don't need to be a crackerjack real estate operator to sell real estate. I'm no lawyer—but I've never had a client to go to jail. Why?

"Everyone is brilliant in retrospect. 'I should have said' is one of the most popular phrases in a human language. 'I should have done'—'I should have known.' Well, I *do* say it, and do it, and know it. I've got an unbeatable library, operating with no timelapse whatsoever. That's all it is, Steve. An instantaneous library and an instantaneous transmission. No mystical aura whatsoever.

"But even you, knowing how it works, are frightened when the system—or an exact duplicate—is directed at you. You can't stand the thought of other eyes watching. I don't mind. Because even my opponent is going to feel a little of that awe. Whereas I am a practical and enlightened man. It's my system, no matter how many times it's stolen. I built it. I *know* it. I know how to use it. And I know how to improve on it.

"I know its weaknesses, and I know where they can be strengthened.

"These people, whoever they are, are out to ruin our reputation and break our monopoly. I don't see how I can stop them, this time. The best I can do is a stalemate, attacking them the same way they have attacked me. But it's not the physical appurtenances that count, in the end.

It's the brain. And my brain is better, and knows more than theirs. They can't win in the end.

"And with that in mind," he concluded, speaking once again to the invisible watcher, "I'm ready to negotiate. May I suggest a meeting with your representatives tomorrow, at noon? Anywhere you wish, of course—since there is no possible neutral ground."

He turned back to Stephenson. "Here, Steve—have an aspirin."

Wilke cleared his throat, glanced around at the flanking members of his staff—Dietz, of course, was among them—and bent his gaze on Henry Walters.

"We are prepared to offer you twenty per cent of the preferred stock in Easyphrase, Inc., together with an assured election to a salaried Vice-Presidency. Mr. Stephenson is offered five per cent and a Vice-Presidency."

Henry Walters picked up his cigarette and inhaled gently. "In return for?"

"Your stock in Spot Dialogue, Inc."

"I see." Henry Walters smiled gently.

"That's a hundred per cent!" Stephenson exclaimed. Wilke and Henry Walters both raised their eyebrows in tolerant amusement. Stephenson flushed and fumbled with his pencil, eyes downcast.

"Now, Mr. Walters . . ."

"Oh, hardly now, gentlemen. I've heard your offer. I'll consider it, and let you know at a later date. I'll consider it," he emphasized, "to myself."

Wilke looked at him angrily. "It was our impression that you were ready to enter immediate negotiation."

Henry Walters nodded. "Certainly it was. Didn't you hear me say so in Mr. Stephenson's presence? It follows that what I tell Mr. Stephenson is not necessarily what I am thinking. And now that I've seen your faces, gentlemen, I shall be going."

He pushed his chair back. He saw Stephenson bursting with enraged vanity. He nodded toward the door, and Stephenson followed.

"You said yourself I was the businessman!" Stephenson exploded in the taxi, goaded beyond his limited endurance. "I'm an equal partner! What kind of a fool do you want to make of me? First you won't let me do the talking, and then you insult me! We've got to present them with a united front! We've got to stand firm!"

Henry Walters leaned back and lit a new cigarette. "Steve, what I said was that you were the business *front*. And, yes, you're an equal partner—I want your interest in Spot Dialogue to be genuine and sincere. But, tell me something, Steve." He faced Stephenson and sent a cold lance thrusting out of his eyes. "Don't you think I could take your stock away from you, anytime I wished? It's still *my* company, Steve. My company, my system, my brain. You know what you are, Steve? When I want you to be, you are my mouth. Just a mouth, Steve."

He sat back and ignored Stephenson's answers, whatever they might or might not have been. Thinking precisely, he took stock.

Spot Dialogue, Inc., was paralyzed. Easyphrase could heterodyne their signals at will. The effect on the client was trauma.

By the same token, Easyphrase had to persuade him to join them before they could operate.

Had Easyphrase thought of some of the other qualities of omniscience?

Probably. Wilke was a shrewd man—not really intelligent, but shrewd.

There was, then, a distinct possibility that Easyphrase might have offered its services to the government. Wilke wouldn't see the inevitable disaster there. He'd see the profits.

Henry Walters had plotted that staircase to disaster a long time ago. First you work for the government. Then the government works for you. Then you *are* the government.

Dominion over the Earth ensues. This places absolute power over everything and everyone in your hands and the hands of your descendants. And then, after two or three generations of making hay while the sun shines, you discover that the human race, adapting readily to having its thinking done for it, has lost all initiative. Result? Your time is spent in desperately trying to maintan the interdependence of civilization—which can only be supported successfully by the interaction of discreet individuals with individual motives. Final result? You still keep your absolute power and gigantic profit—but you count that profit in flint arrowheads. And, after a while, you can't even get the parts that maintain the machines that maintain *you*.

But Wilke wouldn't see that. He couldn't begin to understand that the hardest part of the discovery of the Walters system had been in deciding where *not* to apply it.

Henry Walters noted in passing that Stephenson had run the gamut from protest through pleading to threats. He shrugged Stephenson's hand off his shoulder and continued his summation.

It followed that he'd accept Wilke's offer. Easyphrase would absorb Spot Dialogue and Henry Walters, much as tuberculosis baccilli absorb a bacteriophage.

Henry Walters smiled slightly, while the cab drew up in front of the Spot Dialogue building. "We're here, Steve," he said gently. "You can stop talking now." His smile broadened. "I wonder what makes you think Wilke will ever believe in our united front now?"

That was Wednesday. On Thursday, Henry Walters came into the office at his usual time, sat down behind his desk, and was about to call Stephenson in when Stephenson knocked on the door. His face was set, and his whole manner was rigid.

Henry Walters raised his eyebrows. "Good morning, Steve. I was about to ask you to come in."

Stevenson nodded curtly. "I thought you might. I've been waiting for you to come in."

"And?"

"Henry, what are we going to do? Have you decided?"

Henry Walters nodded. "But, for obvious reasons, I can't yet tell you what my decision is."

Stephenson nodded. "That makes sense. Look—I've thought of something, too. And it's the kind of plan that can be talked about. Maybe it's the same one you've got—I don't know. But I'll outline it anyway."

Henry Walters smiled slightly, but he nodded. "Go ahead."

"Okay. We fight. We give them back tit for tat. We'll keep them off balance, and meanwhile we'll get the government in on it. It'll snarl us up in legislation and investigations from here to breakfast, but, in the end, we'll win. Maybe win some juicy government contracts while we're at it. How's that?"

Henry Walters smiled. It was a neutral smile. Let Stephenson parade his pipe-dreams for the rest of the morning, if he wanted to.

Stephenson grinned. He was a fleshy man, and the grin was fleshy.

"Henry, did you know that the tips of your ears get red when you lie? Did you know that you consider tolerating an untruth a lie? Did you know that you have a compulsion toward truth and infallibity? Did you know that you would like to be God?"

"What?"

Stephenson grinned inexorably.

"Your background—your parents, your environment—were all rigid. You were taught right and wrong. When you tried to disguise wrong, you always gave yourself away—because you *knew* right. And you knew you should be punished for your wrong. Did you know that? Easyphrase knows that. Easyphrase has quite a library."

"Steve. . . ." Henry Walters said slowly, "How long have you been an Easyphrase client?"

"Since last night. Not client. Major stockholder. I've sold our stock to them. Ours. Not just mine. It wasn't hard, once I was told how to unlock your directorate."

"Steve. . . ."

"And now that we know for sure you didn't intend to fight, we know for sure that you intended to join us and bore from within. So I'm not at all sorry I'm doing this to you."

Henry Walters broke the lances of his eyes on Stephenson's artificial armor.

He took a deep breath.

"We're liquidating our furnishings," Stephenson told him. "Please get out from behind that desk."

He took another breath. Then he laughed. He looked at Stephenson, and saw him frowning at the laughter.

"Okay, Steve," he said.

It was going to be a tough haul. Easyphrase would have their eye on him night and day. But they couldn't liquidate his mind. Okay.

So he couldn't be God anymore.

He wondered how he would do as Lucifer.

DIPLOMATIC COOP

by DANIEL F. GALOUYE

> Daniel Galouye has had many fine science-fiction
> stories published, and the best of them have showed
> a single pattern. He is good at all kinds of science-
> fiction, but he is at his flavorful peak when he takes
> a standard science-fiction gimmick and stands it on
> its head. Everyone knows scores of stories in which
> aliens from outer space conquer Earth. It takes a
> Galouye to seek out the mirthful other side of the
> coin—where Earth sends out missions to the aliens,
> pleading to be conquered.

"But we're not Malarkans!" Secretary of Commerce Munsford's hands executed an impatient gesture that was lost
in the vast office.

The official behind the desk scrutinized Munsford and
the Secretary of Interplanetary Affairs. "Malarkans are
always playing tricks like this."

The Secretary of Commerce straightened with con-
straint, forcing an exaggerated degree of dignity that was
complemented by his thin gray hair. "This is no trick,
sir."

"We're Solarians," explained Bradley Edgerton, right-
eously taking exception. "To be more exact, we're—"

"You look like Malarkans to me," the official grumbled
unbudgingly as a weight on his desk levitated and
thumped itself back down to emphasize his skepticism.
The humans tried not to stare. He was full of tricks like

that. "It'd be just like them to try to kick off a wild *vataar* hunt for some imaginary world."

"To be more exact," the Secretary of Interplanetary Affairs continued doggedly, "we're Solcensirians—a composite word for we who inhabit three systems, Sol, Centauri and Sirius. We have until very recently been unaware of the Greater Galactic Community."

The official leaned back, his bulging, many-faceted eyes staring through the distant wall. One of the tendril-like growths on his forehead vacillated. It was a summons. At once an assistant materialized beside the desk.

"Run a check on three systems called Sol, Centauri and Sirius," the official ordered. "I want complete data on position and date of initial contact." The assistant nodded and vanished.

Edgerton gripped the desk. "But you won't find them listed! That's why we're here. We want to get registered for trading privileges."

"Toveen tells us we have a wealth of raw materials that's in extreme demand," Edgerton added eagerly. "And there's so much we can gain from contact."

He stared through the wall that became transparent under the imperceptible pressure of a glance. And, visibly awed, he surveyed the towering spires and curving ramps and vast precincts of Megalopolis—a city that made even the most advanced Solcensirian metropolis look like a hick town.

The official glanced up questioningly. "Who's Toveen?"

Munsford relaxed, satisfied that finally the conversation had taken direction. "Toveen is an independent trader. He plotted a new course through one of our systems and encountered a Centaurian ship."

"He told us about the Community," Edgerton continued, "and placed his High Galactic linguistic assimilator at our disposal. He also brought us here in his ship."

Munsford spread his hands impatiently. "Now will you register us?"

"Oh, I couldn't do that," the official said sharply. "This is only the Racial Traits Division of the Department of Galactic Coordination. You'll have to go to the Bureau of Trade Compacts, I suppose."

Megalopolis was vast and wonderful and completely

covered the surface of Centralia—a stark edifice of colossal proportions symbolizing the triumph of Galactic Man over his stellar environment. It was a place that accommodated the representatives of a thousand diverse races. It was a wonderland of fantastic color and crisp efficiency, of sprawling parks and magnificent fountains, tall buildings and grandiose statues—all products of a technology that meager Solcensirian science couldn't even conceive.

To Munsford, it was a composite of awe-inspiring might and polish. It left him numb.

Edgerton, chin in hand, was staring sullenly out the window of the surface car as it glided effortlessly over the elevated, high-speed ramp.

"We don't seem to be getting anywhere, Andrew," he sighed. "Knocking around from office to office, trying to find the right door to get our foot into—"

The Secretary of Commerce gripped the other's shoulder. "We're going to succeed," he said with determination. "We've got to. There are ten billion people back home, all waiting for the bright new era to start."

Edgerton laughed mirthlessly. He ran a hand over his bald head, shining in the warm, friendly glow of Centralia's vivid orange sun. "Funny. That's how I look at it, too. We're like a tribe of prespace savages just come into contact with civilization and patiently waiting for all the marvels of science and culture to descend upon them."

Then he stared soberly at Munsford. "Suppose we're not accepted?"

The driver, a loosely dressed man with baggy, faded clothes and a cherry-red face that abounded with exotic features, turned half around.

"You'll be accepted—if that's what you want," he prophesied.

Munsford leaned forward. "But suppose we can't qualify, Toveen? What if they won't have us?"

Toveen laughed. "They'll register you when they find out about all that carbon and silicon."

"I suppose," Munsford agreed, "it *is* just a matter of finding the right office to get the ball rolling."

The driver sent the vehicle in a tight climb up a ramp that spiraled endlessly around a towering needle of a building. He braked it in front of an imposing high-level entrance.

"I think this is the Bureau of Trade Compacts." He followed them out and punched the autocontrol stud, sending the car off to park itself. "Wait here; I'll make certain."

Toveen disappeared through the arched entrance and Munsford and Edgerton moved closer to the gleaming metal wall so they wouldn't obstruct traffic boarding the mobile pedestrian strip.

The strip, the Secretary of Commerce marveled, was an incredible triumph of mechanical science. Although it was unbroken and endless, it somehow slowed almost to a stop before the entrance, yet maintained undiminished speed approaching and receding from the building.

His gaze left the strip and wandered fascinated upward along the ramps and spires and lofty buildings that obscured the sky and plunged the streets below into dense shadows.

The Secretary of Interplanetary Affairs nudged him. He looked around, suddenly aware that he had been gawking like a back-planet bumpkin. He shrank self-consciously before the amused stares of several Megalopolitans.

Edgerton gestured awkwardly toward the audience they had attracted. "We must be acting like satellite dwellers on their first trip to New Terra."

"As Solcensirian diplomats," Munsford agreed, "I suppose we ought to do a better job of shaking the hayseed out of our hair."

He wondered whether their cutaway coats, striped trousers and suede gloves, in contrast to the colorful and imaginative clothes of those all around them, weren't contributing to their outlandish appearance.

Edgerton glanced down at his cane and spats. "Let's face it, Andrew," he said dispiritedly. "It's going to be difficult to maintain any appreciable degree of dignity on Centralia."

"Someday we'll belong here, Bradley," Munsford promised. "Someday Solcensirian representatives will circulate in Megalopolis with as much sophisticated indifference as the next Galactic citizen."

There was a rending crash.

Munsford stared down over the edge of the landing

terrace. Two passenger cars had collided on a ramp far below and had left a jumbled, twisted wreckage commingled with the almost-mutilated bodies of their occupants.

Traffic ground to a halt as an official vehicle swooped down from the heights and disgorged men and equipment. Crushed bodies were taken from the crumpled steel and laid on stretchers. The litters were covered with dome-shaped metal lids; dials were twisted momentarily, then the lids were removed.

Dazed casualties rose from the stretchers and walked unsteadily over to a waiting convalescent car.

"God!" Munsford marveled. "We couldn't achieve that degree of medical technology in another ten thousand years!"

Someone tapped him on the shoulder. "Credit check, please."

He turned. Facing him was a uniformed man with chitinous skin and curiously misplaced arms that seemed more like prehensile flippers.

"I beg your pardon," Munsford said densely.

"Credit check—to see that no counterfeit certificates are in circulation," the official explained, giving him a quick flash of a badge. "I'm a spot-check investigator for the Department of Authentic Monies."

"Oh." Munsford feigned comprehension. "What do you want?"

"I've got to inspect your currency. Let's see your credits."

He backed off a step. A device resembling a check-canceler on spindly legs materialized on the landing before him.

Munsford and Edgerton emptied their billfolds and handed over the credits Toveen had advanced them.

The inspector fed the bills into one end of the device. It clicked, mumbled and flipped them out the other, stacking and wrapping them. He handed the packages to the Solcensirian delegates. The machine purred gently, flashed a green light and vanished.

"Everything's in order," the official offered as he stepped onto the pedestrian strip. "Enjoy your stay."

The mobile sidewalk whisked him out of sight.

"Say!" Munsford exclaimed. "You don't suppose. . .?"

He looked suspiciously down at his packet of credits.

But Edgerton had already unwrapped his bundle. Discarding dignity for the moment, he swore and exhibited the sickeningly blank sheets of white paper.

Toveen strode from the building. He saw their expressions and glanced knowingly at the worthless slips. "Boys, you've been taken good."

"Thief!" Edgerton shouted. "Police!"

"Won't do you any good," Toveen said. "They'll just politely explain that civil protection doesn't extend to nonregistrants. Come on, this is the Trade Compacts Building."

The clerk across the counter could hardly be called even humanoid. His predominant features were somewhat saurian, including reptilian eyes and thick-scaled hide.

"That's correct," he verified. "The Bureau of Trade Compacts supervises intercourse between the various systems and clusters."

Edgerton was visibly relieved. "Then we *do* have the right place."

He laid his cane and gloves on the counter. "Mr. Munsford and I represent a tri-stellar system composed of five worlds rich in vast reserves of silicon, carbon, potassium and ferric compounds. Among our exportable products are. . . ." He quickly warmed up to his subject.

Munsford, meanwhile, reflected with some concern over his disappointing experience with crime in Megalopolis. But then he chided himself on his gullibility. Of course he shouldn't have been carried completely away with the shining veneer of the Galactic Community.

So crime *hadn't* been entirely weeded out of the ultimate culture. So vestiges of it *still* existed. So what? From a universal standpoint, crime was nothing more than the prerogative of devious individual activity—noncomformity. And, as such, it must be an inevitable concomitant of intelligence.

Having thus rationalized the anachronism of vice in Utopia, Munsford found it easier to realign his philosophical sights on the finer facets of Galactic civilization —undreamed of science and technology, marvels of transportation and communication, the incredible degree of medical advance and—

"Yes, we're quite proud of our cultural level," the clerk suddenly interrupted Munsford's thoughts. Munsford gulped. The clerk looked away, embarrassed. "I'm sorry. But you were beaming out, and I was carried away with the intensity of your thought pattern. . . . Now, Mr. Edgerton, what were you saying?"

Munsford stared respectfully at the saurian, wondering how many Galactic races were telepathic. Then, as he studied the clerk more closely, it suddenly occurred to him that beneath the alien features he could sense the presence of incredible wisdom such as would accrue only to a species marvelously long-lived.

"All Galactic species are long-lived," the Saurian explained. "But our longevity isn't inherent. The life-span of the average newly-contacted candidate culture, we find, can be artificially increased at least ten times."

Munsford felt humble and awed before the revelation. For himself, who had already lived the greater part of his life, it would probably mean little. But for his grandchildren—for the billions of young and newborn. . . .

"To begin with," the clerk was telling Edgerton, "I must point out that all cargo will be subject to assessment in the amount of fifty-six per cent of value payable in Galactic currency or seventy-one per cent in commodities deliverable."

Munsford started. "Fifty-six per cent! Seventy-one per cent! That's pretty steep, isn't it?"

"Come now, sir. It costs a great deal to coördinate the life-stream of Galactic commerce, to administer the needs of ten thousand cultures."

The Secretary of Commerce relaxed submissively. Of course, it must be expensive to run the Galaxy. Actually, it was ridiculous to think that he should have overlooked the possible existence of trade taxes and tariffs and charges for governmental services. Lord knows the costs were high enough for the administration of Solcensirian affairs!

The clerk rubbed his claws together. "Now, if you'll let me see your certificates of registration and incorporation we'll set the wheels in motion."

Munsford backed off. "But that's what we're here for—

to register and become incorporated into the Community!"

The saurian straightened indignantly. "I'm sorry," he snapped. "There's been a misunderstanding. We can't process any compacts until you're officially registered."

Irritated, Edgerton fidgeted. "Look—we've been to five offices already!"

But the Secretary of Commerce accepted it philosophically. Naturally the official routine and exasperating delays would be proportionately magnified in comparison with the meager and primitive Solcensirian government. Yet, you'd imagine that with an administration as evolved as the Galactic Community's in Megalopolis, some way would have been found to reduce the red tape.

"I'd suggest you get an early start in the morning," the clerk proposed, "and try the Department of Contact, Survey and Recordation. That's the normal avenue of entry."

The meal of delicacies from remote regions of the Galaxy was still a heavy feeling in his stomach as Munsford settled lethargically in a contour chair in the Transient Quarters' recreation room.

Edgerton and Toveen strode across the lobby from the dining hall and dropped sluggishly into chairs on either side of him.

"You fellows certainly are stubborn about this registration business," the old space trader offered phlegmatically. "If it'd been me, I'd have gone home long ago."

The Secretary of Commerce glanced over at Toveen. "You don't seem to be sold on Galactic culture. Why?"

The other shrugged. "Every man to his own taste, I always say. For me, it's too complicated. When you boys pay me off for putting you in contact with Megalopolis, I'll have what I've been looking for."

"Are you sure," Edgerton asked, "that you'll be content with a subsidized estate on New Terra?"

"What more could I want?"

Even on the five Solcensirian worlds, Munsford realized, there was always the occasional misfit—the malcontent to whom civilized existence represented an endless succession of complications and impositions. Even on Terra there were those who withdrew to themselves and lived simple lives in the hinterlands. And New Terra would merely be Toveen's hinterland.

Various walls of the recreation room had seemed to melt away and now they were like windows looking out on vast and magnificent scenes of other worlds. The dioramas were both weird and beautiful as they pictured settings of unimaginable variety.

Only then did Munsford begin to appreciate the scope of the Galactic Community and the miracles of executive processes that must be required to maintain order and calm.

He leaned toward Edgerton. "I'd certainly like to sit in on one of Megalopolis' lawmaking sessions, wouldn't you?" he asked, reverting to the Solcensirian tongue.

The Secretary of Interplanetary Affairs slumped in his chair and frowned. "I wonder if we could begin to understand their parliamentary procedure. It must be totally different from our concept of government."

Munsford nodded soberly. "It would probably make the principles of our Constitution look like a savage tribe's rules for headhunting."

Edgerton shook his head wistfully. "Imagine the total elimination of pork-barrel politics. No wrangling over legislative rules. No sneak measures. No rider bills. No patronage maneuvers, spite legislation or partisan antics."

The Secretary of Interplanetary Affairs sighed and rose. "We'd better turn in. With a little luck we might wind up our mission tomorrow."

Munsford seized his arm. "Know something, Bradley? I've just about decided we're not getting anywhere because our attitude is wrong. We're suppliant, self-conscious, overwhelmed by the wonders all around us."

He rose and meticulously straightened his cutaway, aligned the seams on his gloves. "We must remember our dignity and our rights. Whether they like it or not, Solcensirian culture is *already* part of the Galaxy. "They've *got* to accept us."

Edgerton drew erect and waved his cane with determination. "By space! You're right, Andrew! We're duly authorized representatives of ten billion people. We—"

A tall, lean man with pale orange skin confronted them. "I beg your pardon. You wouldn't know who I am, would you?"

Munsford eyed him severely. Back home, this was one of the stock approaches for a handout.

"No, we wouldn't," Edgerton said, also aloof. "Why should we, my good man?"

There was distress in the robed figure's face. "I've got to find someone to identify me. I've mislaid my credentials; they won't admit me before the Grand Council. And that's the only chance I've got to keep them from talking our bill to death.

"Unless, perhaps," he went on garrulously, "we can strike up a deal with the Popaldanian Cluster by supporting their measure for construction of six thousand new spaceports."

"You've got to keep them from talking *which* bill to death?" Munsford asked, still wary of another swindle.

"The bill to prevent them from forcing twenty-foot spatial segregation on the Clarkians."

Munsford squinted. "Who are the Clarkians and why would the Council want to segregate them?"

"A hundred and three trillion citizens of the Clark Cluster. We're telepathically receptive over a twenty-foot distance. And I don't think it's fair. Why should I, the Prime Minister of a whole cluster, have to stand at least twenty feet away from you just because I can see, for instance, that you spent two weekends on an orbital yacht with a young lady a month before you were elected to your first public office?"

The Secretary of Commerce coughed explosively and his face flushed almost as crimson as Toveen's. He glanced at Edgerton, then backed away from the Clarkian.

Director D'Loon of the Department of Contact, Survey and Recordation was quite agitated. Twice Munsford's height, he presented an awesome and imposing appearance as he paced in his office.

"Impossible!" he declared. "Utterly impossible!"

Munsford squirmed.

"One world we might have missed," D'Loon continued vindictively. "But a vertiable budding empire of five worlds—"

He left the thought hanging on a note of profound concern and dropped into his chair.

"I think I can clarify it," Toveen offered. "Sol, Centauri and Sirius are in Sector Fourteen-Yellow."

The Director's face twitched with sudden comprehension. "The Backwash Area! But it was established thousands of years ago that every stellar body in Fourteen-Yellow is Larmanian Triple-Z in type—incapable of developing intelligent life of even the lowest order."

"Quite obviously your survey was incomplete," Edgerton said impatiently. "Now, will you consider our application?"

Sour-faced, the Director absently fingered miscellaneous articles on his desk. "Naturally we'll have to. But just what the procedure will be, I don't know. I should imagine there'll have to be some sort of an interdepartmental hearing."

More red tape. Munsford fought down a growing feeling of despair.

D'Loon's hands made an explosive sound as they flopped down on his thighs. "We shall see. At any rate, I don't want to lose track of you two. I'd hate to know there's a burgeoning culture somewhere in the Backwash Area and have to spend three or four thousand years looking for it."

"This hearing," the Secretary of Commerce asked. "When will it be held?"

"As soon as possible."

Munsford briefly contemplated months going by.

D'Loon smiled. "In the meantime you can be planning your official offering."

Munsford stared at the Director. "Offering?"

"A customary courtesy extended to the Community by all neophyte cultures. You might look on it as an admission fee. It needn't be much—say, twenty-five years' output of your top ten commodities."

Munsford glanced painfully at Edgerton and Toveen. The space trader's smug expression was a reminder of his warning that things in the Greater Community were often complicated and frustrating.

"Who would ever have thought that Fourteen-Yellow would eventually produce?" D'Loon said abstractedly, rising. "Let me show you something."

He led the way across the room to a huge metal door.

Scintillating light flared out from the frame as he turned the knob.

Hesitatingly, the two diplomats and Toveen followed him through into a simply furnished room and out onto a veranda cloaked in the moist, dark stillness of night.

It was quite evident that they were no longer on Centralia. Overhead, an unimaginably dense splash of unfamiliar stars shone brilliantly—like a miniature galaxy.

"Apparently this is your first experience with the telemitter," the giant D'Loon observed. Then he indicated the magnificent sweep of stars. "The Backwash Area, as seen from Taddolp VI, on the fringe of Sector Fourteen-Yellow. Seventy-four million suns and not a one of them worth a damn except yours."

Munsford looked back enthralled at the veil of pulsating light that filled the inner doorway. From Centralia to God-only-knew how far away *in the space of a single step!* And, back in the Solcensirian sphere, travel from Terra to New Terra was still a matter of almost two years!

He was sure now it wouldn't be difficult to convince the Solcensirian government that even fifty years' production of their top ten commodities wouldn't be too steep a price to pay for just one article of Galactic technology —the secret of the telemitter.

Munsford and Edgerton were caught up in the fascination that was Megalopolis. So absorbed did they become in exploring the architectural wonders, the incredible scientific achievements, the dynamic and unimaginably developed culture, that they were like children in some impossibly fabulous fairyland.

And soon the Secretary of Commerce found himself wholly occupied in arranging the order of priority in which the features of the ultimate fairyland would become realities of the Solcensirian worlds. First, of course, they would have to have the telemitter. Next, the secret of longevity. Then a completely new repertory of medical techniques. And perhaps telekinetic ability could be acquired.

The list of marvels grew rapidly and reached imposing proportions so quickly that Munsford soon realized it would take a special commission of Solcensirian scientists years to absorb the magnificent technology of the Galactic Community.

The two diplomats were still expanding their list three days later when the courier from the Grand Council arrived at Transient Quarters with the summons.

He delivered it on a shining metal platter as a retinue of rigidly uniformed musicians trumpeted a fanfare and Council attendants unrolled a lush carpet on which they strode to the vehicular corridor. There a luxurious air car awaited.

They were whisked off, skimming the tallest spires of Megalopolis, while an escort of determined, smaller craft orbited around the larger ship with sirens screeching.

Munsford leaned back against the plush upholstery contentedly. Protocol had caught up with them. At last they were being accorded the formal courtesies due them as diplomatic representatives of ten billion potential citizens.

The flight to the hearing chamber was short since, ironically, the building to which they should have gone in the first place was less than a mile from the spaceport.

Another carpet was unfurled from the craft to the entrance and the trumpeters blasted their ears with a jubilant flourish as Munsford and Edgerton, heads high, strode amidst a cordon of dignitaries. Banners fluttered from cornices of the building; a band played a triumphal march, and thousands flanking the entrance cheered lustily.

Toveen arrived belatedly in an aircab and exhibited a congratulatory grin, indicating he would wait outside.

The hearing chamber was cavernous, with an immense domed ceiling. Munsford and Edgerton were ushered to a dais and all around them government officials sat at great curving tables.

A most dignified elderly man in a flowing robe and with a noble mane of thick, white hair rose and a respectful hush fell over the assembly.

"Greetings," he intoned gravely. "Through its President, the Grand Council extends a cordial welcome to you as representatives of your people. And we are pleased to announce official acceptance of Solcensir as the newest member of the Great and Cooperative Community."

Munsford stood with head bowed and eyes closed. The Solcensirian worlds had made it. They were in.

What did it matter that they would have to pay the Bureau of Trade Compacts a fifty-six per cent assessment on cargo offered? Or that the five worlds would have to provide the Department of Contact, Survey and Recordation with an admission fee of twenty-five years' production of their top ten commodities? Solcensir was *in* and that was all that mattered.

A haggard individual who looked almost human rose at the table designated "Department of Labor and Productive Statistics."

"What is your population?" he asked.

"Ten billion," Edgerton answered proudly.

"And the working force?"

Munsford raised a finger thoughtfully to his temple. "Why, about half of that, I should imagine."

"Twenty per cent of which figures out to one billion. We shall expect you to make the selections and have them registered."

Munsford frowned. "Registered for what?"

"Employment in Greater Community sub-bureaus and departments. Usually we require thirty-five per cent. But that's after a century's membership. The Community must be adequately represented on the constituent worlds, you know."

Edgerton leaned forward suspiciously. "Who bears the cost? Who pays the wages?"

"The member worlds of course. You wouldn't expect the Community to foot the bill for services you receive, would you?"

Munsford's shoulders sagged. Fifty-six per cent of cargo offered he could explain. And he could even justify twenty-five years' production of ten commodities. But this . . .

"How soon can we send in an assessors' team?" It was a diminutive, elflike man at the Property Department table who had posed the question.

Munsford swabbed his brow with a crisp handkerchief. "Assessment team? You don't mean . . . ?"

"My dear sir, you are obligated to support the administration of the Galaxy to the extent of five per cent tax annually on all real and personal property."

Munsford drew protestingly erect. "Now wait a minute. I—"

Someone rose at the Bureau of Better Breeds table. "Will next month be too early to send in a team of geneticists?"

The Secretary of Commerce's mouth seemed to be hinged permanently open now and his handkerchief was quite moist.

"We expect total cooperation," the official went on, "in elevating the Solcensirian population to Galactic standards."

He approached the dais, alternately scrutinizing the two diplomats. His gaze eventually steadied on Munsford. "Offhand I'd say that if there are many of your general type, considerable culling will be in order."

"Now see here! I—"

Edgerton gripped his arm. "Quiet, Andrew."

The President confronted them. "Apparently you gentlemen haven't been amply informed of the obligations which neophyte cultures are expected to assume once the Greater Community contacts them."

"No, we haven't," Edgerton quickly confessed, pressing his handkerchief to his forehead. "But we are anxious to find out. And we will most certainly be eager to satisfy all requirements."

Munsford stared protestingly at him. "But, Bradley! You don't—"

"For God's sake, Andrew," the other whispered. "Shhh!"

Someone popped up at the Surface Configurations table. "We'll expect you to supply accurate cartographic documents on the land masses of all planets in your system in order that we may coördinate a defense network."

"And there's the matter of the Galactic draft," added a spokesman at the Manpower Mobilization table. "Your requirements in this department are ten per cent of all eligible males, five per cent of the females and two and a half per cent of the neuters, if any."

"What's all this about a defense network and draft?" Munsford blurted, dropping his handkerchief. "Is there a war going on?"

The President laughed. "Of course there isn't. And we intend to see that it stays that way. But only total preparedness will discourage the Andromedans. You understand that, don't you?"

"Of course we do," the Secretary of Interplanetary Affairs said enthusiastically, winking at Munsford. "And we shall be honored to contribute our share."

The Secretary of Commerce, finally catching on to Edgerton's strategy, reiterated, "We certainly shall."

The Defense Department spokesman was on his feet again. "Splendid. Then you'll understand why we have to be ceded one-fourth of all land masses for fortification purposes."

"But," Edgerton asked solicitously, "you'll let us provide for upkeep of the forces, won't you?"

The official smiled. "Only to the extent of four-fifths of the cost. The Greater Community pays the rest."

A familiar figure rose at the Department of Contact, Survey and Recordation table. "And now," D'Loon asked eagerly, "where did you say the Solcensir Empire was located?"

"In the Backwash Area," Munsford answered eagerly.

"We know that. But there are seventy-four million suns in that region. What are the exact coordinates of Sol, Centauri and Sirius?"

"Oh," said Munsford innocently, "Toveen has that information. He found us, you know. We'll have to get it from him. He's outside now."

Arm in arm, Munsford and the Secretary of Interplanetary Affairs started up the aisle.

The huge room settled down into a drone of casual conversation and the President leaned back in his chair, folding his arms patiently.

"We'll be right back," Edgerton called over his shoulder.

And Munsford added under his breath, "—like hell!"

Centralia dwindled to a pea-sized disc, hidden in the brilliance of the backblast, as Toveen's cargo ship slipped into the untraceable regions of hyperspace.

Suddenly concerned, the trader asked, "This hasn't queered my chances for that estate on New Terra?"

"On the contrary," Munsford reassured, "we'd like nothing better than to have you as a permanent guest.

That way you won't be likely to tell anybody where Sol-censir is located."

"But," Edgerton quickly qualified, "you'll have to include the ship in the deal."

"Now, boys," Toveen chided. "If I wanted to keep out from under the nose of the Contact Bureau, I wouldn't go gadding about the Backwash Area on Cosmic Drive."

Munsford straightened disdainfully. "After we get home this ship is going to go gadding unmanned and in only one direction—directly sunward."

Toveen nodded. "I see," he said. "Well, excuse me."

He engaged the autocontrol circuit, rose, stretched, glanced casually at the two diplomats, and stepped aft into his cabin.

He locked the door.

He listened for a second, then, satisfied, pulled a suitcase from under his bunk. He threw back its lid, exposing a metal chassis cluttered with electronic parts and knurled knobs.

"Toveen calling," he said softly.

Pause.

"This is Toveen calling," he said with some asperity.

There was a click and a whisper from the suitcase. Then a voice as soft as his own said, "Report, Toveen."

"We're leaving Andromeda now," he whispered, one eye on the door. "We're heading back for their own galaxy. They want to destroy this ship."

Hesitation from the suitcase. "Well," said the voice cautiously, "that *is* a problem. We won't be able to come in and rescue you."

"Rescue? Hell, I *want* to stay there. It ought to be an easy life. And, you know, looking at a galactic civilization through their eyes, I began to feel the way we wanted them to feel. I think I'll like the quiet backwoods life on New Terra."

The voice coughed warningly.

"Oh, don't worry," Toveen said easily, "I won't say anything against our Andromedan civilization. Except, of course, to them. For them I'll keep on dropping little hints about the fierce and unpredictable Andromedans."

The voice cautioned: "Don't overplay it, Toveen. We don't want them getting second thoughts and deciding to join the mythical Galactic Federation after all. . . . Well, I guess this is good-by, Toveen. We'll miss you." The voice assumed a ritual chant. "In the name of the Andromedan people, you are commended on the successful completion of your mission. The three hundred and thirteenth Galactic culture has now been successfully indoctrinated to avoid attempts at making contact with other cultures, thus permitting us Andromedans to remain at peace. Your sacrifice has not been in vain. The people of the Andromedan systems wish you well." And the voice clicked off.

Toveen, grinning widely, shut the lid, locked the suitcase and shoved it back under the bed. It was his only contact with his home civilization in the Andromedan nebula. He paused thoughtfully. Then, thinking of telepathic saurians and the ubiquitous con-men of the world where he had grown up, he took it out, opened the lid and picked up a hammer.

In half a minute, he had reduced it to powder, chuckling to himself all the while.

THE SCENE SHIFTER

by ARTHUR SELLINGS

It is a well-known fact in editorial offices: American science-fiction writers have the scope and excitement, but their English opposite numbers own the insight and the wit. Like most well-known facts, it is riddled with more exceptions than one can count; but for proof of the second half of the proposition, Arthur Sellings reliably delivers perception and pleasure to us all.

This man was named Boyd Corry—the deed had been done by his press-agent, not his parents—and he was perfectly normal for a fading movie star, except for one thing. He thought the world was out to get him.

He wandered one night, as he had done many nights, through the downtown fog. He never said what it was he was looking for, but it was perfectly simple—he needed to be reassured. He needed to discover incontrovertibly that he existed and that he was loved. What it took to prove this was an old movie of his own.

In a second-run theater on a side street he found what he needed: An image of himself, twice as large as life and haloed in neon lights. He lurched into the lobby.

Cradled in the darkness inside, drugged by a travelogue commentary, he closed his eyes. His chin sagged. He slept. Then, like a Dalmatian responding to a fire alarm, his sleeping self heard the blare of trumpets that announced the opening credits of his motion picture and dutifully shook him awake. He sat up eagerly, in time to see the monumental letters that blazed on the screen:

ONLY ONCE IN ETERNITY
starring
BOYD CORRY

Tears started to his eyes.

That picture was all of three years old. Things had been different then, hadn't they? Everyone at his feet. Before they'd seen what a selfless guy he was and had ganged up against him. Well, he'd shown them. Let them kick their heels for a couple of days. That might give them time to learn that the star was still the man who counted —not these jumped-up producers and directors.

And the public was on his side. *A-ah,* feel that stir in the audience as on the screen he came galloping over rolling greensward—as he swung, doubleted, lithely from the saddle.

This was what made everything worth-while. His public understood. They knew that the real artist crucified himself for their sake—for the sake of their dreams. It was the gossip columnists who didn't understand—the narrow-nosed skunks.

The sense of injured virtue generated a maudlin glow that bathed him lovingly. Then he began to grow impatient, angered by the unbridgeable discrepancy between the face he saw there and the one that gaped at him every morning out of his shaving mirror.

He started to his feet, but dropped back, frowning at the screen. The frown deepened into a scowl. He shook his head dazedly and stared again.

Something was wrong.

The scene on the screen was not the one *he* had acted in. Impossible!

Then it dawned on him. They were getting at him again, the mangy tribe of columnists and jealous rivals and soulless executives. The ones that were always trying to get between him and his loyal public. Well, they weren't going to get away with this.

He jumped to his feet, waving his arms wildly. "Turn it off! It's all wrong! It's a fake!"

Faces turned up whitely in the flickering darkness. Peo-

ple started to *sssh*, to yell back at him. The burly shadow
of an attendant did a clumsy fandango along the row toward him.

"Turn it off!" Corry raved. "They're cheating you, I
tell you!"

The attendant reached him.

Twenty seconds later, Boyd Corry, no longer protest-
ing, was being dragged like a sack up the aisle. A minute
after that, the manager, who had picked up the phone to
call the police, took another look at the profile that lolled
against the back of a chair in his office. His eyes widened. Then, shaking his head sadly, he dialed Mammoth
Studios.

"But *why*?" Cavanagh lamented. "If you have to cut
loose, why the hell don't you come over to my place? You
can get as drunk as you like there!"

"But you don't understand, Vince," Corry whined, wiping a clammy forehead with a trembling hand. "They're
getting at me again."

Cavanagh's sigh exploded like a swearword. *"They!*
Can't you get it into your handsome fat head that nobody's
getting at you? Everybody's *for* you." He knew that
wasn't exactly true, but he also knew that the few hundred
people who would like to see the paranoid star toppled
from an already shaky throne were not in league with each
other. Not yet, anyway.

Corry laughed hollowly. "Oh yeah? Well, I saw it with
my own eyes. They're wrecking my pictures."

Cavanagh looked tired. "This one's been around, hasn't
it? A few feet always get scratched and have to be cut
out." He turned to the manager. "Isn't that so?"

The manager nodded.

Corry glared at him. "It wasn't just cutting, and you
know it." He turned back to Cavanagh. "I tell you, that
picture was being murdered. It's a plot to make me look
ridiculous."

Cavanagh looked at the manager, who shook his head
blankly. Cavanagh nodded in sympathy.

Corry, stirring, caught the glance. "So you don't believe me either? Well, I can prove it. You ought to know
the film. You scripted it, didn't you?"

"I scripted the first version," Cavanagh agreed.

Corry persisted, "You remember that bit near the beginning where I'm fighting the Duke of Anjou's mercenaries?"

Cavanagh rolled his eyes heavenward.

"Well, remember where I vault over the battlements and kill four men with one sweep of my—my—"

"Halberd?" Cavanagh prompted gently.

"That's right," Corry said eagerly. Then his face became savage. "In the version I just saw I miss the lot of them and fall flat on my—" He spluttered. "It was humiliating!"

Cavanagh turned to the manager. "Did you see this scene?"

The manager shifted feet. "No, I was busy out front. And this is the first day we've run the film. But there can't be anything wrong with it. It came through the usual channels."

"He's lying," Corry yelped.

Cavanagh waved him down but, to placate him, asked the manager, "Is there a chance that a wrong reel could have slipped in?"

"It's extremely unlikely. Of course, I can check."

"But it was *me*," Corry broke in. "Well, a double. It's a deliberate plot."

"All right," Cavanagh sighed. "Either you dreamed it, or there *was* something wrong with that reel. Will it satisfy you if I check it personally?" His eyes sought and received assent from the manager.

Corry scowled. "They've probably changed it by now."

Cavanagh's thin face registered sudden vehemence. "Of all the twisted paranoid— All right then, go ahead and believe there's one huge conspiracy against you. In that case, there's no point in my checking the reel. I wash my hands of it. And if I ever hear any more nonsense out of you, there *will* be a conspiracy against you. And I'll be the one leading it."

Corry squirmed. "Don't say that, Vince. You're the only true friend I've got." His eyes were pleading. "You will check that reel?"

Cavanagh smiled a sad and inward smile. "Okay, but let that be the end of it." He went to the door, opened it and beckoned outside. A genial tough rolled in. "Here,

Mike, take Mr. Corry home, will you? And he said he'd like you to stay by him tonight."

Mike grinned. "Sure thing, Mr. Cavanagh." He hoisted Corry up and planted him on his feet in one effortless gesture.

Corry twisted back. "All right, Vince, but you'll tell Drukker?"

"Only if there's anything wrong with that reel," Cavanagh called after him. He nodded to the manager, and they went up to the projection room. He examined the reel for a minute, then handed it back with a sigh. "Sorry about all that," he murmured, and tipped the projectionist a five dollar bill.

He went out into the night air, pondering sadly.

So it was that Simon Drukker, chief of Mammoth Pictures, was left untroubled by the affair—for a week.

Corry adopted what he called a "lofty disdain" toward the episode. In fact, his subconscious stored it furtively away as yet another item in the card-index of persecution with which he would confront his enemies the day that they went too far. As for Cavanagh, he bought the latest book on paranoia.

Then the call came.

Cavanagh and Corry both happened to be in Drukker's expensively stark office. When Drukker made the substance of the call profanely clear, Corry gave Cavanagh a look of triumph.

"Anyway, why bother me with it, you raving idiot?" Drukker was roaring, when Cavanagh tapped him on the shoulder.

"I think you'd better be bothered," Cavanagh cooed. "This isn't the first time."

Drukker glared, barked into the phone that the matter would be seen to, and slammed the receiver back. He turned to Cavanagh. "And why wasn't I told?"

"And get that reception? Anyway, I didn't believe it either." He told Drukker briefly of the episode of a week before. He was conscious of Corry's gloating over his shoulder.

The star elbowed in. "You see, somebody *is* getting at me." (The enemy within was craftily calculating Drukker's pretended ignorance. A query in red went against his name.)

Drukker only snorted. "Don't overestimate yourself. You're not in every picture this studio turns out."

"You mean——"

"Somebody is getting at Mammoth." Drukker's bulk rose from the chair with surprising swiftness. "And that's *much* more important."

Drukker, Cavanagh, Corry and Mike tumbled out of the car and almost collided with the manager who was jittering on the sidewalk. It wasn't the same cinema, Cavanagh noted, but it was in the same district and the same kind of small neighborhood house.

"Something awfully screwy's going on," the manager blurted. "I've seen this picture five times. It's one of my favorites. But——"

Drukker pushed brusquely past him. The other three tagged on.

Cavanagh's knowledge of the picture was limited to having seen a few scenes in production, but it needed no previous acquaintance at all to realize, in a very few seconds, that there was something odd about it. Something decidedly odd.

For one thing, it was obviously designed to be a drama, right in the middle of the Stanwyck-Crawford-Wyman country. Coming from Mammoth, which had no claims on any of those estimable ladies, it featured Esther Fenn, with Allen Blaikie setting up the nasty situations for Esther to emote in.

At least, he should have been; but this was being played strictly for laughs.

Cavanagh was conscious, even in the darkness, of Drukker's purpling. Yet the audience seemed to be enjoying it.

For himself, he had to admit that it was a lot more entertaining than the usual Fenn-Blaikie opus. Surely in the original version Esther, when she came across the bottle concealed by her alcoholic husband, would have struck her famous fold-arms-stroke-triceps pose, the code symbol for furious thought? She seemed about to do just that. Instead, she stopped, gave the audience a conspiratorial leer, then uncorked the bottle and helped herself to a generous swig.

The audience roared.

They roared even louder when Esther elegantly burped.

A strangled noise came from Drukker. *"Turn it off!"* he spluttered.

"But it's nearly over," the manager said, alarmed at what such an action might provoke.

It was. In came Blaikie, catching his wife taking a second swig. He calmly reached in his coat, brought out a gun, pointed it at Esther and pulled the trigger three times. She expired on the carpet.

What must have been the original score was still grinding out turgid chords in the background as the face of Allen Blaikie looked out of the screen. "Nobody," he said, "steals my booze and gets away with it."

The music mounted to a crescendo. It was THE END.

The audience seemed to agree. They were still laughing as the lights came up. Drukker was already barging out of his seat, carrying all before him.

Cavanagh and Corry followed him up to the projection room.

"That's the one," Mike said as Drukker burst in. He nodded to a reel.

Drukker grabbed it, scanning the last footage at a rate that sent celluloid snakes writhing all over the confined space. A dumbfounded look spread over his large features. He handed the reel to Cavanagh as if in a bad dream.

And Cavanagh jumped at what he saw.

As far as he had thought it out, there had been a switch of reels—whether for a hoax or for darker reasons. Yet—*the frames he was holding were obviously the right ones*. There was a midget Esther stroking her triceps like mad.

Which meant—

He looked at Drukker. Drukker's small eyes became even smaller as they came to rest on the operator. "Cavanagh, call my lawyer. Get him here right away. Nobody leaves this place until I find those phony reels."

"Oh, yeah?" protested the operator. "I'm a union man. Either I get double time or—"

"You'll get it," Drukker snapped. Then, disgusted at his own magnanimity, he added menacingly, "Which may not be the only kind of time you'll be concerned with before I get through here."

Some time after two o'clock, Cavanagh and Drukker returned wearily to the latter's offices. With them was Braun, the lawyer, a sharp-faced man with bushy black eyebrows. They gave him a top-heavy look. Corry had been sent home with Mike when Drukker had realized two things: first, that the star's powers of solution were limited; second, that he was due on set at dawn for the last shots of his current picture.

"Well?" Drukker demanded as soon as they were inside. "When do I start getting some answers from the brains it costs me a small fortune to hire?"

Cavanagh turned from pouring a large whiskey. Braun patted his briefcase smugly. "Well, there's at least a dozen counts we can sue on. Libel, infringement of copyright and trade mark, fraud—"

Drukker almost howled. "That's a fat lot of good when we don't know who's doing it!"

"Well, this one instance isn't anything to go haywire over," said Cavanagh.

Drukker snorted. "Hasn't it penetrated that bone head of yours that this could be the end of Mammoth?"

"Exactly. But every time it happens will be one more chance to find out how it's being done."

"Yeah? We didn't get very far this time."

"Perhaps," Braun put in soothingly, "your technicians will find out something when they're putting that projection room back together."

"Well, if they didn't find anything when they took it apart, I don't see—"

The telephone bell cut across Drukker's speech. He grabbed it. After a few seconds he put it back. "That," he announced stonily, "was the technicians. They didn't find a thing."

"Well," Cavanagh observed cheerfully, "then the interference doesn't come from the projection room."

"Then from where?"

"From the audience. It's pretty obvious, isn't it? If anybody was tampering with the projection system, the manager would have to be in on it, wouldn't he? So why should he call you? No, it must be somebody in the audience."

"But that's fantastic!"

"So was what we saw tonight," Cavanagh reminded him.

He shrugged. "Though heaven knows how it's done, or how anybody could make an apparatus portable enough."

"So what do we do? Frisk everybody when they come out?" Drukker's voice was scathing.

"No, nothing as crude as that. Just get camera apparatus fitted at every ticket-office of every cinema in town showing our films, so that a shot is automatically taken of everyone who buys a ticket. Sooner or later the number of faces common to each repetition of tonight's performance will narrow down to one—or one group, if it's a gang doing it."

"But the cost!" Drukker wailed.

"Can you think of anything better?" Cavanagh asked him.

It took Drukker sixteen hours to decide that he couldn't. Even then, it took another incident the very next evening to convince him. It happened at yet another cinema, and the report he got back really had him shuddering. What had happened to an ordinary light romance woke horrible visions of the studio's being closed by the police for making indecent pictures. He signed the authority for the necessary apparatus with a sweaty hand.

In the next fortnight four more cases of tampering were reported and shots of the cash customers duly rushed to the studio. By that time Drukker had learned something which went a little way to easing his torment.

Whoever was doing it wasn't carrying on a vendetta against Mammoth alone. One by one the other major studios were finding themselves up against the same baffling problem.

Rumors began to fly. Cryptic notes started to appear at the foot of the film columns. The police raided one cinema, on a complaint of indecency, but found nothing.

Meanwhile the narrowing-down process went on. The first set of films yielded eight hundred and thirty-seven faces. The second set, sixty-one definite, and five not so definite, common with the first. The third, though it ruled out the five not-so-definites, showed up stubbornly with forty-three. *"Real fans!"* Drukker commented disgustedly.

But the last one, an afternoon performance, really narrowed the field down—to five. Drukker was all for acting and straightaway pouncing on all of them. Braun managed to restrain him with a reminder of what four damage suits could cause.

And then the next report came in. Drukker summoned Cavanaugh, Braun, Crowe and Philp, together with Mike and a strong-arm squad.

The shots arrived. Drukker personally ran them through the projector. Minutes passed. One shot after another was passed over. Then one matched. Drukker marked the film strip, then started off again. The number left dwindled. A strip only inches long was left, then— the screen glared whitely.

Drukker ran back to the marked shot.

"That's him," he announced. "The enemy. Everybody take a good look. Right, let's go."

On the way to the picturehouse, leading in one of three long black cars, Drukker made gloating noises from between cigar-clamping teeth.

"I'll teach him to monkey with Mammoth," he proclaimed to the world in general.

Cavanagh stirred. "But it's not just Mammoth any more. I don't get why—"

"Why I treat it as my personal pigeon?" Drukker chuckled. "I've always been a staunch defender of the film industry's interests, haven't I? The others know I've got a lead on this. I'm sure they'll recognize the value of my efforts." He chuckled again.

Cavanagh grimaced, knowing what that chuckle meant. Drukker was seeing a fat profit in the deal.

"Another thing," Drukker said grimly. "The scheming skunk got me first. I'll have a personal satisfaction in shaking the truth out of him."

Cavanagh said nothing. He was thinking of the face they had just seen on the screen, thinking that Drukker sounded ridiculously melodramatic, talking like that about a little old man with a monk's tonsure of white hair, who looked as if he wouldn't harm a mouse. . . .

In the flesh he looked even smaller, frailer. His cheeks were pink and innocent as a child's. Drukker spotted him as the crowds streamed from the cinema.

They pounced.

The little man looked up, startled.

"I'm Mammoth Pictures," Drukker told him. "I made that picture you've been tampering with."

The little man started to expostulate, then shrugged resignedly. "Well?"

"I think you owe us a visit, don't you?"

"Do I? Oh, I see. Ah—tomorrow morning?"

"Right now."

"But—my landlady. I always—"

"We'll call your landlady," said Drukker, steering him into the foremost car.

The little man sat awkwardly in the canvas bucket with a hole that some expensive designer had called a chair. He looked up at the faces that ringed him.

"First," said Drukker, "your name."

"Alfred Stephens."

Drukker nodded expectantly. "Now—how do you do it?"

The little man hesitated, then smiled slightly. "I don't know."

"*What!*" Drukker's huge fists clenched. "Now look—"

"No, I mean it. Believe me, I don't know."

Drukker took a grip on himself. "All right, we'll let that one ride. What do you use?"

"Use?"

"What do you do it with?"

"Why, nothing."

Drukker spluttered. His eyes sought the strong-arm squad—A blue-jowled member lumbered over. Braun coughed nervously. Cavanagh slid in front of Mr. Stephens.

"Now—let's all remember that Mr. Stephens is our guest. I'm sure that if we give him time to express himself—"

"Thank you," said the little man, with a composure striking in one so frail. "If you will be good enough to point out to this gentleman that intimidation will not help, I will do my best to oblige."

Drukker growled, met Cavanagh's eye and subsided. He gestured to the goons to remove themselves to the anteroom.

"That's better," the little man said. "Now. You will understand if I speak with a certain reserve. I ask you to imagine a man who has been, all his life, a lover of the cinema. Let us imagine that he often gets impatient with what is offered him for his entertainment. He has seen films become more and more stereotyped, you understand?"

"Go on," Drukker said heavily.

"Well, it's true, isn't it? Oh, those cobwebbed situations, that weary old dialogue!"

"Do you know how much it costs to make a picture?" Drukker shouted, stung. Cavanagh grinned.

"Then they might as well be made properly," Mr. Stephens said reprovingly. "Now, where was I? Ah, yes. Our critical friend begins to get discontented with a film. He starts thinking how it could be, and then—it happens."

When Drukker became intelligible he was saying, ". . . trying to tell me the film goes off the rails because you *think* it off!"

Mr. Stephens clucked. "Because *he* thinks it off. The man I'm talking about."

Drukker looked helplessly to Philp and Crowe. The two technicians closed ranks as if for mutual protection. Two pairs of shoulders rose and fell weakly.

"It *could* be," Cavanagh put in, "some form of telekinesis."

"Tele—*what*?"

"Telekinesis. Moving objects at a distance by the power of thought. Remember *The Poltergeist*? I did research for that. Cases are pretty well authenticated of people's moving heavy vases, things like that. So why not somebody being able to move a collection of shadows on a screen?"

"But the sound's changed, too."

"Is that any harder?"

Drukker shook himself like a Labrador coming out of water. "No, it's too fantastic. I'm not going to believe it."

"Thank you," said Mr. Stephens promptly. "I'm glad. If that's all, then—"

He started to rise. Drukker, coming to, pushed him back.

"All right," he snarled. "I believe you. Now listen to me. You're a nuisance in any cinema you enter. More than that, there's evidence that you've changed some films into—well, they'd never have got by the Hays Office like that."

The little man's cheeks became a shade pinker. "Ah yes. Well, perhaps our friend's imagination did run rather wild."

"Then he'll have to stop it, won't he?"

"Umm. Well, perhaps. It's not that he's of a particularly sensual nature, you understand? But love scenes on the screen do get tediously unreal, don't you agree? Even in Theda Bara's day they were wearing a bit thin, but at least there was *something* then."

"I didn't mean just the love scenes," Drukker told him heavily. "I meant all of it."

The little man looked at him regretfully. "But our friend can't help it."

"In that case," said Drukker, "he'll just have to stop going to the movies."

The little man returned his gaze steadily. "But that's out of the question."

"Is it? We'll see about that. My attorney here says that you can be sued on at least a dozen counts already. If you play ball with us, then we'll play—" He jerked irritably. "Yes, Braun, what is it?"

"Intent," Braun whispered urgently in his ear. "None of those charges would stick if we couldn't prove intent."

"But you told me—"

Mr. Stephens had sharp ears. "You'd need proof, too," he interrupted blandly.

Drukker scowled. "All right, Mr. Stephens. What's the price?"

"Price?"

"For staying out of picturehouses for the rest of your life."

"Oh. Dear me, does everybody have a price in your world? I'm sorry, but my annuity is enough for me. And I haven't any relatives living. In any case, I thought I had made my interest in the cinema clear enough. Nothing is worth sacrificing that for."

The look of chagrin on Drukker's face was suddenly replaced by a quite lifelike geniality. "Well, I can make you a happy man. A preview of every picture we make —right here at the studios. And any picture from any other company, I could arrange that. A car to pick you up. One of our starlets to keep you company. How's that?"

Mr. Stephens sighed. "Well . . . no, I'm sorry, but that wouldn't be the same thing at all. It's not just the picture, you see, but . . . well, the atmosphere, the feeling of being one in a crowd, sharing the experience of hundreds of other people, the—yes, even the crackling of candy papers."

"Candy papers!" Drukker raised his hands and dropped them wearily.

"Perhaps," Cavanagh observed dryly, "you could offer Mr. Stephens a job as director. From what I've seen of his abilities—"

Drukker had started to glare. But now, suddenly, he was laughing. He shook the little man's hand jovially, hoisting him to his feet at the same time.

"Well, that's all right, Mr. Stephens. If we can't reach agreement, then we can't. And it's skin off nobody's nose. Glad to have met you. And good night."

The rest looked on blankly as Drukker ushered a slightly bewildered Mr. Stephens to the door.

"Take Mr. Stephens home, Mike," Drukker called out. "Good night again, Mr. Stephens."

He closed the door on the little man and turned back benignly to the rest of them.

Cavanagh spoke quickly: "Listen, you're not going to—"

Drukker looked pained. "I'm not going to do anything. Except to see that our friend has a bodyguard from now on. If he ever goes near a picturehouse, Mike, or whoever's on duty, will just tip off the manager. It's as simple as that." He surveyed them with the air of a mother hen rebuking her brood. "So I don't know what everybody was getting so steamed up about."

Cavanagh found the house—a modest rooming-place downtown, and paid off his cab. Mike was lounging against a lamppost, picking his teeth.

"Any sign?" Cavanagh asked.

"Hasn't shown his face once." Mike stirred morosely. "This private eye stuff gripes me."

Cavanagh nodded sympathetically. "Enjoy your lunch?"

"Huh? Aw—" Mike threw away his toothpick disgustedly. "Just trying to kid myself. I don't get a bite till Louie comes on at two."

"I'll take over, Mike, till then, how's that?"

Mike beamed. "Gee, thanks, Mr. Cavanagh." He lumbered off, but turned. "Don't forget to ring Drukker if you move—"

"I won't, Mike. *Bon appetit.*"

As soon as Mike was out of sight, Cavanagh went up the steps and rang the bell. The door was opened by a birdlike woman. He had just asked for Mr. Stephens when the little man himself came down the stairs. He had a topcoat on. "Oh, hello," he said when he saw Cavanagh. Cavanagh thought he sounded rather tired.

"Remember me—Cavanagh? Mind if I tag along?"

"Won't you be doing that anyway?" the little man asked with a wan smile.

Cavanagh nodded. "You worked that one out?"

"It didn't take much working out. Ah, this way." The little man sighed as they started off down the street. "What else could he do? I didn't need to look out of the window this morning and see that palooka down below."

"I'm not his relief," Cavanagh thought it wise to explain. "Well, only voluntarily. Drukker looks on you as just a menace. But for me—well, I couldn't sleep last night for thinking about that gift of yours. I'd like to know more about it."

Mr. Stephens turned a quizzical eye on him. "Did Drukker tell you to say that?" Then, seeing the look on Cavanagh's face, "Sorry. What do you want to know?"

"For one thing, has it only recently shown itself?"

"Well, I've an idea I've done it before—but only in snatches, so that I didn't know at the time. You realize it wouldn't be so easy to know. But looking back now I guess that—no, I *know* that it happened before. But not so anyone would notice. Even me."

"And films are all you can move? Nothing else?"

The little man chuckled. "Levitate furniture, you mean? No, only films. I've never dabbled in anything out of the ordinary."

"Out of the ordinary?" Cavanagh's eyebrows rose. "What do you call what you can do, then?"

"Anything psi, I mean. That's what they call it, isn't it?

Anyway, perhaps it isn't so strange that it should happen to me. I'm a shy man. Worked all my life alone in a dispensary. Never married. Lived all to myself. Films are the only abiding love I ever had. I guess my will has got more and more focussed on the screen—much more than most people's."

"Mmm," Cavanagh pondered. "But that still leaves it a mystery."

They walked along in silence for a time, then the little man said, "Well, there's one thing—" He hesitated.

"Yes?" Cavanagh prompted gently.

"Well, I guess that what a man thinks decides what he can do. And I think a lot—philosophize, if that's not too grand a word for it. Shy men are great philosophers. They're really rationalizing away the chances that they lose to the—the—"

"The Drukkers?"

"I guess that's what I mean. Anyway, I was always impressed by what old Plato said—about all the world that men see being no more than a lot of shadows thrown on a cave wall."

"And the men who see them?" Cavanagh said quietly.

"I don't know." The little man smiled. "Just shadows with eyes, maybe. And don't ask me what the fire that casts the shadows is. That's going a bit deeper than I ever wanted to. But that way of looking at things is a big consolation to a man who never really amounted to much in his life. It tells him that all the things that people strive for—money, power, possessions—are only shadows."

Cavanagh suddenly felt the loneliness of Mr. Stephens and his courage. The courage that faced up to the limitations of the being that housed it—the courage that could stand up to Drukker as the little man had done the night before. Cavanagh wasn't used to expressing his true sentiments, not after ten years in Hollywood. But he said now, hesitantly, oddly shy himself, "But . . . you *have* amounted to something. This gift, surely, is something wonderful?"

"Maybe. Thank you for saying so." He shrugged and seemed about to say something more, but stopped. He stopped walking, too.

Cavanagh looked up. They were outside a picturehouse. It was very much like—yes, it was the very place where Corry had made that scene.

That had only been a few weeks ago, but it seemed an age now. Somehow the little man with the strange talent seemed to have introduced something wider—something of the eternal—between.

"I was going to the pictures," Mr. Stephens said. "Coming in?"

Cavanagh shook his head sadly. "I hoped you wouldn't make it difficult for me."

"Ah, yes." The little man fixed grave eyes upon him. "But Drukker doesn't have the last word, you know. You see, if he tries to stop me, I shall simply give my story to the newspapers. They've already, I believe, got on to the fact that something odd has been going on. I think they will listen to me."

"But would you want that? The publicity and everything?"

"Frankly, no. But it would be worth it to beat Drukker."

"But what good would it do?"

"Only that. I told you I'd never had any experience of psi powers. There are plenty of people who have. They've evidently never thought of altering movies. If they have, I haven't heard of it. Think what *they* might do if they knew it could be done. Like the four-minute mile."

Cavanagh went suddenly pale. "*No!*" He grabbed the little man by the arm. "You don't know Drukker. Do you think he'll stand by and see his whole world tottering about his ears?"

The little man looked down, pained, at Cavanagh's restraining hand. Shamefaced, Cavanagh let him go. The little man started to move toward the ticket-office.

"You fool!" Cavanagh shouted wildly. "I'll have to call him."

"If you have to," Mr. Stephens said, turning. He looked sadly on Cavanagh. "I thought you had more guts."

Cavanagh stood there a long moment. Then he hunched his shoulders and called Drukker.

Drukker's reaction was immediate—and just what Cavanagh had feared it would be. Suddenly he knew that he had to get the little man out of danger.

He paid for a ticket with trembling hands and hurried inside.

The night scene was on the screen.

Outlaws, by the look of it, closing in on clustered wagons. The auditorium was dark. The usherette seemed to be engaged elsewhere. Cavanagh groped his way, cursing, down the aisle.

Then his eyes adapted to the dark.

The cinema was sparsely occupied, and quiet. He suddenly knew that the little man hadn't started operating. He felt a vague unease. He told himself not to be a fool, that that didn't mean a thing. Then he saw him. In the middle of the third row, his tiny figure hunched up in his coat.

Cavanagh started toward him—and jerked as the screen erupted noisily. Guns went off like lightning flashes. Cavanagh reached the little man—and stopped. His hand stretched out as if someone else was moving it.

The outlaws had attacked. Drukker's goons would have no need to.

Little Mr. Stephens, his head lolling sideways, was dead.

"Well," said Drukker, turning to Cavanagh and Corry as they ducked the last flash-bulbs and entered their box, "this is all *our* picture tonight, eh?" He chuckled as he settled into his seat. "You know, little Mr. Stephens could have been a real nuisance."

Corry beamed. The affair had had the strange effect on him of stilling his paranoid fears. By demonstrating that people plotted against other people than himself, the fact had registered on his subconscious that not everybody could therefore be plotting against *him*.

"Uh-huh," Cavanagh said. It was two weeks now since Mr. Stephens' sudden death; the inquest had returned a verdict of heart failure. Cavanagh had gone right out and bought a new book, on the guilt complex.

The lights dimmed.

The usual hubbub of a premiere died down, and Cavanagh resigned himself to the usual agony of a new Boyd Corry epic.

At least, he thought in an effort to make it bearable, *Corry certainly throws himself into a role.* It was almost as if he believed in this technicolored world of plaster turrets and knights-at-arms, strutting and i'faith-ing as if he thought he really *was* the Black Prince.

But the effort was drowned in a returning tide of revulsion. It was just that—Corry's posturing and faked-up athletics—that made the whole spectacle insufferable.

If only—

He stiffened. On the screen the Black Prince was leaping onto his horse. *But he never reached it*. He missed the stirrup completely and fell flat on his face in the mud.

There was a sudden startled titter from the audience.

Then a gale of laughter swept the auditorium. For a moment Cavanagh's world lost certainty. Had they had the wrong man in Mr. Stephens? So that the little man's story had been a pack of lies? And then he realized—

What had the little man said that last afternoon of his life? That he'd tell the papers . . . that people hadn't thought of it before . . . that it was like the four-minute mile; once people knew it could be done. . . .

But no, that couldn't be it. There hadn't been anything in the newspapers. But had he *told* anyone? Yes, that was it—he'd told somebody . . . wakened in them a latent power.

And then the truth impinged—shockingly.

He had to get out. Drukker and Corry were both gaping at the screen. They didn't notice when he got up and made for the door.

For he had realized—it was just as the little man had said—the first time you weren't sure. He hadn't been for a moment—but he knew now. He had another's experience to draw on. Mr. Stephens *had* told somebody—

Him!

HAIR-RAISING ADVENTURE

by ROSEL GEORGE BROWN

A young Louisiana housewife sat down to a type-writer one day last year to find the answer to a question: Was there anything hard about writing science-fiction stories? The answer, it turns out, is "no"—provided you have the wit, the talent and the grace of Mrs. Brown. Because of the idiosyncrasies of publishing schedules, this may not be the first of her stories to see print, but it's the first she sold— and STAR is proud to present it to the world.

Sam had been a bachelor for many years. He liked it. He might have remained so all his life, if it hadn't been for a girl named Ruth. The study of paleolinguistics had kept him happy until then; but Ruth's face and figure began interposing themselves between Sam's eyes and his beloved microfilms. It was a research problem which had to be solved. He solved it by marrying the girl.

Then he learned the facts of life.

This occurred some weeks after their return from their honeymoon. Ruth was knitting, on no evidence, little pink things. Sam was, as usual, working on deciphering some ancient Scythian script, new examples of which had recently been unearthed in lower Russia.

"Sam," Ruth said, in the tone of a wife who has just given a man a good dinner and let him relax long enough. "Sam, *why* do you spend all your spare time fooling around with that silly old stuff? Who cares whether you can read it or not?"

"My daddy always told me," Sam replied without looking up, "that if a thing is worth doing at all, it's worth doing well."

If a man's wife won't tell him things, who will? "Dear," Ruth said gently. "Dear, did it ever occur to you that maybe it's not worth doing at all?"

This jolted Sam. He removed his glasses and put aside his microfilm viewer. "No, Ruth," he replied, feeling vaguely around his person for cigarettes and matches. "No. I've never thought of that. Why isn't it worth doing?" He never did locate a cigarette, but Ruth had so upset him he forgot about it and began chewing absently on the end of the pencil instead.

"Dear," Ruth said, removing the pencil and inserting a cigarette in his mouth, "you work hard all day at the Freight Depot and then you come home and work hard half the night deciphering some old script or other. And for all this your income is less than the milkman makes."

"But my work on epigraphy is for the sake of . . . of scholarship. Of learning. My daddy always told me money wasn't important."

"Sam," Ruth said, taking his hand and patting it soothingly, "Sam, I wish I wasn't the one to have to tell you this. But money *is* important."

"It is?"

"Dear, you really shouldn't have stayed a bachelor so long. You've been sort of, well, cut off from the practical aspects of life."

"But Ruth, you told me that money wasn't. . . ."

"Not for *me,* Sam. Though I wouldn't mind. . . ." Ruth's voice trailed off as she looked meaningfully around the dingy little apartment. "It's the Little Ones that may come along."

"Little Ones?" Sam echoed, frowning as he pictured an invasion of midgets.

Ruth held up her knitting with a coy smile.

"Oh, I see what you mean. You mean *we* might— well." Sam turned pink and had a slight coughing fit. "Doesn't it take longer than that? I mean, we've only been married three months. It really hadn't occurred to me. About any progeny, I mean."

Ruth laughed reassuringly. "Oh, no. Not yet. I was just giving an example of why money is important."

"And epigraphy is not?" Sam was beginning to get his back up a little.

"Not for children, no."

"I don't know why epigraphy shouldn't be important for children. I should think it would be of great benefit to the burgeoning intelligence."

Ruth burst into tears. "I almost hope we don't have any children. What kind of father would you make, with your nose always in a microfilm machine and not caring if we all starve?"

"Are you hungry, Ruth?" he asked anxiously. When she ran from the room and flung herself on the bed, Sam stood around frowning and trying to make some sense out of the whole conversation.

A lesser man might, at this moment, have abandoned his hobby in the interests of domestic serenity. Had Sam been a lesser man, this hour of decision might have left the world balder. As it was, Sam, bent over his microfilm machine in all his spare time, was woven into that fantastic chain of events of which he was the last to be aware. . . .

Sam's evenings with ancient Scythian script were soon curtailed. Ruth, finding the direct approach a total failure, tried the subtle approach. There was company over almost every night. Ambitious young couples jockeying their way bravely through the traffic jams of life, their chins jutting into the wind.

The husbands were only momentarily stunned by Sam's occupation. "Great room for big thinking there," they would say. "You take an office like that, streamline it, get rid of the deadwood. Boy, you'll be appreciated. Take a place like you're in, use a little efficiency, and it'll show, all the way down the line. And when they ask who did it, boy, you just step up and say, 'Me.'"

"But I didn't," Sam would say with a confused frown. "I like my job the way it is. It leaves my mind free. What I'm really interested in is epigraphy."

"Taking a flier in the hog market?"

"No, no. Reading ancient scripts. Writings. You know,

trying to figure out writing that no one's been able to translate."

Ruth had finally given up trying to be proud of her husband's epigraphical accomplishments. She'd finally just switch on the TV when it became obvious that Sam was not going to get interested in vacuum cleaners or selling insurance or advertising or whatever the eager young husband of the invited couple was engaged in.

"Sam," she would sneer, "wouldn't know a good idea if it hit him in the head."

Ruth heard of Sam's Discovery the way most wives find out what their husbands are doing—by listening to them talk to someone else at a party.

"New hair oil?" he was saying. "Nothing new about hair restorers. I've just translated a recipe that works very well. Doubt if you'd be able to stack yours up against it. And this one is almost twenty-four centuries old."

"Yeah?" the young man answered skeptically. He smoothed his well-oiled hair. "Of course, we're careful not to come out with the blank statement that Full Head actually *grows* hair. But we do say that people who use Full Head have more hair, more luxuriant hair, than people who do not. And more people with more hair use more Full Head than any other product. Furthermore, we're prepared to back that statement with statistics."

"It is remarkable," Sam said, "that anyone could think up a statement like that in the first place. I doubt if that could be written in an inflected language. But tell me, where did you get your statistics?"

The young man looked a little sheepish and lowered his voice. "Well, don't let this go any further. These statistics are a side line of a well known Educational Psychologist. It's the same forty New York school children who learn to spell words written in red chalk three times faster than words written in white chalk."

"Well," Sam said, "I don't know how well my recipe would work on New York school children. But it grew hair on the ancient Scythians in 450 B.C. and it grew hair on me on June 22nd this year."

"You're not really serious, are you?"

"Absolutely."

"*That* hair?"

Sam looked uncomfortable. "Well, I didn't say it grew pretty curls. It grows whatever kind of hair you had to start with. I imagine it's a simple chemical that stimulates some hormonal activity or other."

Ruth backed around to observe the top of her husband's pate.

"Sam!" she cried. "It really isn't bald any more. You've actually grown hair!"

"Yes, yes," Sam said impatiently. "What's so fascinating about that? The night I broke the Scythian alphabet, all you did was yawn in my face."

"But you told me all there was written in Scythian were a few old laundry tickets."

"I meant they were mostly lists of supplies and epitaphs and things like that. This recipe just happened to be among them. Probably chiseled into the rock by some shipping clerk."

The young hair-oil man was by this time perspiring with eagerness. "Quick," he said, "tell me. What was in this recipe?"

"It's taken internally," Sam said. "A drink. You use mare's milk, a plant which was probably the same one the ancient Greeks called moly, and white wine. Probably any wine would do."

The young man was clutching Sam's arm and leading him off. Ruth was following, still dumfounded.

"The plant," the young man panted. He licked his lips. He could hardly go on. "What is it? I mean, what do *we* call it?"

Sam frowned thoughtfully. "Afraid I don't know. I've never had any botany."

Ruth let out a long breath. "Thank God. Sam, you fool. Don't you know what you've got hold of?"

"It's that plant with the little white flower that opens just in the morning. You know, they use it on the Morning Joy ad. A very common herb." Sam ignored his wife's noises of admonition.

"I know," the young man said, beaming like a day-old chick, though his hands were still shaking.

"Moly is a very interesting plant," Sam said. "It was the ancient equivalent of Miltown, if you're familiar with that drug."

"*Familiar* with it! That's practically all I can eat."

But the conversation was interrupted by the thud of Ruth's body on the floor.

Sam picked her up apologetically. "Afraid this sort of kills our evening," he said. "My wife has a tendency to nervousness. Especially about epigraphy. But this is the first time she's ever fainted when I started discussing it."

The young man pocketed his hands, after popping a pill into his mouth. "Mind if I come along with you?"

"No, indeed," Sam answered. "So few people show any interest in my work. Would you like to hear how I broke the Scythian alphabet?"

"It sounds absolutely fascinating," the young man said. He hailed a taxi and held the door while Sam bundled in with his wife. "But first, a minor point. How many people know about this recipe for growing hair?"

"At the moment, no one but you and me. And Ruth, if she was listening. You don't know how refreshing it is to find someone else who is interested in ancient Scythian."

Ruth was sitting up, groaning. "You ten-karat jackass," she told Sam disrespectfully. "He's interested in your hair restorer. Don't you know that's worth a million dollars? And you've gone and *given* it away. *Given* it."

"Is that true?" Sam asked the young man, suspicious for the first time.

"Well, I'm interested in the hair restorer *and* in epigraphy. Tell me, are there many people who can read ancient Scythian?"

"You see," Sam told his wife triumphantly, "he *is* interested." He turned back to his new friend. "I am the only person in the world who can read ancient Scythian. But let me tell you how I broke the Scythian . . ."

"Yes, yes," the young man said. "I'm very anxious to hear all about it. But first—have you made up any samples of this hair restorer?"

"Oh, I have half a milk bottle full," Sam replied impatiently. "Why do you care? You don't need it. Let me tell you how I broke . . ."

"Look!" the young man said desperately, as one who abandons the last vestige of his pride. He yanked off his toupee. It was apparent, in the dim light of the taxi, that he was not such a young man after all.

"Oh, all right," Sam said. He extricated Ruth from the taxi. She was in an actual paralysis of rage. "Come on up and I'll give you a sip of this moly mix. Now, the first inkling I got that I might actually be on the trail was when I got the microfilm of a fragment with what appeared to be a picture of a Persian king carved into it and half a word underneath. Now this might have been many names. Darius, Xerxes, Artaxerxes . . ."

"Sam," Ruth said hoarsely, when he had arranged her in a chair, "don't give it to him. There's still a chance."

"Don't be ridiculous, my dear," Sam said. "I've just had my article on the subject accepted. The king was Xerxes."

"No, no," Ruth went on. "I mean the hair restorer."

"Oh, I'd forgotten that," Sam said. He fetched a milk bottle. "Don't know how clean this is," he told the young man. "I don't think Ruth really scrubs them. But I don't have a cold."

"Germs don't bother me," the hair oil man replied. "If you'd just help me get it to my mouth." He had a handkerchief wrapped around his hand, but it was still too unsteady to hold anything. "How long does it take to start working?"

"Oh, I'd say about four hours. I mean, for the fuzz to just start showing. It takes much longer for the hair to grow to normal length."

The young man looked at his watch, sat down and sighed deeply. "Now tell me about how you broke the Scythian alphabet."

"Be glad to," Sam said eagerly. "Now take a look at this fragment." He handed the man a microfilm viewer. "Now, you would probably assume that the name incised under the picture is Persian transliterated into Scythian. Right?"

"The first thing I thought of," the young man agreed. He was running a trembling hand over the smooth skin of his head. "Persian, of course."

"Ha!" Sam cried. "Not at all. You can try it for yourself, if you like. It won't work."

"Then I don't think I'll try it. What did you do then?" He was concentrating on his watch.

"Isn't it obvious? I transliterated the Persian into Aeolic Greek and then again transliterated it into Scythian script. And there it was! I was on the trail of the key to the Scythian script."

"Marvelous." The hair oil man got up and began pacing the floor. "Sorry, but I just can't sit still. My nerves are bad."

"I felt the same way," Sam said enthusiastically, "the night I broke the Scythian alphabet. Couldn't sleep all night. It *is* exciting, isn't it?"

"I think I feel a prickling on my scalp!"

"It's almost unearthly," Sam agreed, "reading something that's been buried all these centuries. I quite know how you feel."

Ruth, who had disappeared into the bedroom, returned with a suitcase in each hand and tears streaming down her eyes.

"Sam, I'm leaving you. I can't stand to stay around and watch this."

"But *Ruth*," Sam said. "You can't do that. I love you. Honestly I do. If you like, I'll give up epigraphy. Now that I've broken the Scythian alphabet I've finished the task I set myself fifteen years ago. No more epigraphy. Now, how's that, dear?"

"Sam, this skin-headed swindler is going to take your hair restorer and make five million dollars out of it, and we're not going to get a damn thing. You don't even know his name!"

The hair-oil man faced her with an expression of bland honesty with an inescapable undercurrent of six ulcers. "Madam," he said, "my name is Chuck Bradford. I have no intention of stealing your husband's formula. I only want to help him. This sort of thing calls for group thinking. Together we can work out—"

"Together, bah! I know exactly what you're going to do."

The door bell rang and Ruth jerked the door open angrily. She backed off, blanching like an almond.

Into the room walked a lengthy, ferocious-looking African native, painted here and there and brandishing a wicked spear.

"Um!" the native said, pointing the spear at everyone in turn. "Who Sam?"

"I am," Sam answered. "Surely you're not from the *Kenya International Epigraphical Review!*"

"Where proof sheets?" the native asked laconically.

"Good Heavens, I had no idea the KIER had that sort of deadline. You can't be the *senior* editor?"

"Where proof sheets?" the native repeated in a menacing tone, shaking his spear and puffing out his painted cheeks.

"Mau-mau infiltration into the KIER," Sam concluded suddenly. "Spies must have sent you."

"Sam!" Chuck Bradford gasped. "You were about to *publish* this thing?"

"On the whole," Sam said complacently, "the article was rather well written. As a matter of fact, it was accepted the first place I sent it."

"Thank God I found out in time!" Chuck said. He popped another pill into his mouth, started toward the native and retreated fast.

"Bwana can't grow hair on shrunken head." The African grinned and poised his spear. It was then that everyone noticed what rattled on the end of the spear. There were two of them, neither in need of hair restorer.

Ruth hit the floor with a thud.

"I'd better get him the proof sheets," Sam said. "If he'll promise to get them to the KIER when he's finished. You promise?" he asked the native.

"Witch doctors use hair grower to be number one place of honor again. Then me give proof sheets to brother number three boy in office of KIER. If witch doctors no eat powerful printed page," he added.

"Then it's not Mau mau," Sam said. "It's witch doctors?"

"White missionary send son U. S. A. medical school, come back, work big magic. Now witch doctor send son U. S. A. witch doctor formula. Work bigger magic. White doctor lose practice. Witch doctor take over."

"And all this over the hair restorer," Sam muttered. "I might have known my article on epigraphy wouldn't stir up this much excitement. Well, I don't care if you have the proof sheets."

"Don't give them to him, Sam," Chuck shouted. "Look at him. He'll kill us anyway."

The native had gone into a light soft-shoe war dance, and the look in his eye was not gentle. He had started singing a jerky sort of song to himself and he was thrusting the spear nearer and nearer to the three white people.

Ruth groaned, sat up, looked at the African and shuddered. "Why the hell don't you do some group thinking?" she snapped at Chuck.

"I am," Chuck answered. "If I could only stop shaking long enough."

"And you, Sam," Ruth sneered at her husband. "What are you going to do? Just stand around and look apologetic while he sticks a spear into me?"

The African evidently had an itchy spear hand and was having trouble restraining himself. "Bwana no get proof sheets? Me find. Bwanas go to happy Methodist heaven. No need hair restorers."

"Wait!" Sam cried. "I'm not a Methodist. Look. I've just remembered I left those proof sheets at the office. You'll have to wait while I go get them."

"Me no wait!" the native said.

"Don't get the police," Chuck yelled hysterically. "They'll have your recipe in all the papers. My God!" he groaned. "I'd rather get hung on his spear than lose this thing now."

"Me go with you," the African boomed.

"I'll be back," Sam said cheerfully. "You two just wait here."

"Don't get the police!" Chuck shouted again.

"Oh, *get* the damn police," Ruth said, sobbing. "Sam, this is the bravest thing you've ever done, getting him out of the apartment like this. Do you want me to c-a-l-l the p-o-l-i-c-e," she spelled, glancing furtively at the dancing African, "after you leave?"

"By no means," Sam said calmly. "Don't forget, dear, that I'm a shipping clerk. I handle invoices from everywhere in town. I know exactly what to do with our elemental friend."

Ruth and Chuck alternately glared at each other, had hysterics, and chewed on Miltown until Sam returned, some hours later.

"Your hair," Sam remarked to Chuck when he walked in the door, "is growing out absolutely gray."

Chuck ran to the living room mirror. "My God, there it is! Real hair! I don't care if it's purple."

"Darling," Ruth cried, throwing herself into her husband's bony arms, "what did you do with Jumbo? And why were you gone so long? I was afraid!" She began to sob, unable to go on.

"I palmed him off on Abercrombie and Fitch," Sam said. "First I went by the shipping office and I faked an invoice on him. Then I called Abercrombie and Fitch and convinced them they had ordered an African bearer with a spear. They had to come out, of course, suitably prepared to deal with him. I showed them the invoice and what could they do? He's their problem now."

"Oh, Sam, you're just wonderful!" Ruth cried, clinging to her husband in abject admiration.

"Damn it," Chuck said. "Now why don't I have ideas like that? An idea like that could make a million dollars."

"Oh, you go away," Ruth told Chuck. "You're not going to make a million dollars off our idea."

"I've already got the formula," Chuck said.

"Well, you might as well take the proof sheets," Sam said. They were flapping in his hand. "But I want them back. I really had left them at the office."

"I just want to look at the directions," Chuck said. He seized the proof sheets and began to copy vigorously into his little black Idea book. After that he abandoned the last vestiges of decency. He grabbed the bottle of hair restorer Sam had mixed up and lit out.

"Sam," Ruth said, "I'm sorry for all the things I've said about you. It was ingenious the way you got rid of that cannibal, or whatever he was."

"It was not ingenious. It was merely a matter of attention to detail. If I had not made an exact copy of an Abercrombie and Fitch invoice, I would never have gotten away with it. You admit, then, that if a thing is worth doing at all, it's worth doing well?"

"Oh, yes, darling."

"And I am capable of deciding what's worth doing?"

"Yes, *yes*."

"But still," Sam went on, like Socrates chasing down some point of logic, "you are sorry about the hair formula. Now tell the truth, Ruth. You still think money is important?"

"Yes," Ruth admitted with the monosyllabic regularity of most of Socrates' pupils.

"And you don't think I'm capable of making money

because all I can do is mess around with the meanings of words, in one language or another?"

"Now, Sam, I didn't say that. I meant that you don't even *try* to make money. Nobody can do it if they don't *try*."

"Well," Sam said, "you just wait and see."

"But Chuck's gone off with your formula. And I know that kind of man. They'll have the thing in full production in a week. Sam, maybe if we rush down to the patent office—"

"Dear," Sam said, "I'm not even going to try."

Ruth didn't turn on the radio, go out of the house or watch television for the next week. The advertising was everywhere. "Full Head positively guaranteed to grow hair! Not more hair! Not less scalp! Just the same hair you had before. The hair of your blazing youth!"

A check for a thousand dollars came from Full Head a week after the meeting with Chuck Bradford. Ruth would have torn it up, except that she now had very good evidence that a Little One was, indeed, on the way.

"*This*," Ruth said, waving the check in Sam's face, "is our share of the hair-restorer money."

"Rather a handsome sum," Sam said, quite pleased.

"Oh, Sam, you're impossible. Do you know what *they*'re making out of it?"

"I don't care what *they* make."

"If I ever get my hands on that Chuck Bradford again," Ruth said gritting her teeth, "I'll—"

The doorbell rang.

It was Chuck.

"Don't do it, Ruth," Sam said. "He doesn't look like he could stand it. He looks like a—" Sam groped for words because Chuck, indeed, looked awful. His new hair hung despairingly over a face now gaunt and haunted.

"Like an old hound dog," Ruth concluded. "You have your nerve showing your face here, Chuck Bradford, after the swindle you pulled on us."

"I have *my* nerve?" Chuck shouted. Then he sat down with his head in his hands. "I don't even have any nerves left. They've all popped from overuse. Sam, you've perpetrated the worst horror since Nero burned Rome. Why couldn't you just have been a pyromaniac or a sex fiend?"

"What on earth are you talking about?" Ruth asked.

"Don't act innocent. You were in on it, too."

"On what?"

"Yeah, yeah," Chuck said. "You got me into this mess, now you get me out."

Sam was looking even milder than usual. "Some hitch in the hair restorer?"

"You bet your sweet life there's some hitch!"

"I was afraid something like that might happen," Sam said.

"What is all this?" Ruth asked. "Nobody ever tells me anything. *Your* hair looks all right, Chuck."

"Oh, yes," Chuck moaned. "*My* hair is all right. I've pulled it out by the handfuls, believe me, and it all grows back. All the people we tried Sam's bottle on grew hair. All the hair anybody would want. And it stayed. There's just one trouble."

"Get to the *point*!" Ruth said. "What's the just one trouble."

"We didn't waste any time," Chuck went on, ignoring her. "We got it into production in a matter of hours. Not days, I tell you, *hours*. Packaging, advertising, everything went out zip-bam-boom! It sold. Boy, it *sold*. Supermarkets, drug stores, hot-dog stands, everywhere. Then, guess what?"

"What!" Ruth screamed.

"The hair all sprouted out for one week and then it fell off. Not just the new hair, mind you, but the old hair, too. I tell you, if something isn't done, you're not going to be able to tell Times Square from a billiard table. And guess who gets the blame for all this? Me. *Me*!" Chuck sprang up and began pacing the floor and chewing on the edge of his handkerchief.

Ruth laughed until the tears ran down her face. "How marvelous!" she said, when she could talk. "How *marvelous*!"

"Sam," Chuck said, going up and clutching his erstwhile friend by the lapels. "Sam, you've got to help me now. You've *got* to. What did you put in your formula that isn't in the recipe?"

"Nothing," Sam said, gently extricating his lapels. "Absolutely nothing else. Only what I told you. Mare's milk, moly and white wine."

"Then *why* did your mixture grow hair that stays and ours doesn't?"

"It ain't what you do," Sam replied, "it's the way that you do it. You probably processed it wrong."

"We followed the directions *exactly*, Sam. *Exactly*."

"That's the trouble. You got the wrong directions."

"You mean you deliberately gave the wrong directions?"

"Nothing of the sort," Sam said indignantly. "When *I* do something I do it right. My daddy used to say, 'Son, if a thing's worth doing at all, it's worth doing right.' "

"You're just torturing me," Chuck said. "Why don't you put bamboo splinters under my fingernails? Let me know right now if you're not going to explain yourself, and I'll go ahead and jump out of the window."

"*I* sent in a correct manuscript to the *Kenya International Epigraphical Review*. There was a misprint in the proof sheet. That was not my fault. Nor was it my fault that you assumed the recipe was correct and used it for your own purposes."

"My God!" Chuck said. "I came to you as a last resort. I didn't really think you'd know what was wrong. Our chemists are working on it night and day. They'll probably come up with a solution in the next year or two, but we can't wait that long. *I* can't wait that long. I'll be lynched. Sam, what is that misprint?"

Sam picked up his microfilm viewer and began looking through it and taking notes on 5x8 cards. "I'm not going to tell you."

"You *know* it? One word? And you're *not going to tell me!*"

"Why should I?"

"Oh, now we can talk business," Chuck said, snatching the viewer away from him. "How much? Five thousand? Ten? Oh, the hell with it. My nerves are shot. We'll go to a million. O. K. What's the misprint?"

Sam retrieved his microfilm viewer and became absorbed in it again. "My daddy always said," he remarked absently to Chuck, " 'Son, money isn't important.' "

"But *Sam*!" Ruth cried, snatching the microfilm again. "A million dollars!"

"How much do you want, Sam?" Chuck asked, pale as a prepackaged mushroom.

"My daddy always said—"

"Never mind," Chuck interrupted. "All right, you freak, money isn't important to you. We'll get you something else. What *is* important to you?"

"Well," Sam murmured thoughtfully. The room was silent for the space of half a cigarette. "Epigraphy is important to me."

"We'll get you all the epigraphy you want," Chuck said, panting heavily. "Tons of it. Miles of it. However it comes."

"It doesn't work that way," Sam said. "There's only so much of it, and it's all free."

"Oh, my God," Chuck cried. "Sam, isn't there *anything* else in the world you want. *Anything* you'll trade that misprint for?"

Sam thought and thought. "Yes. There is something else I want. But it isn't the sort of thing you could do for me."

"Full Head can do it. Full Head would sell human souls to correct the recipe for that hair restorer. What is the thing you want?"

"Oh, it would sound silly to you."

"No, it wouldn't." Chuck grabbed Sam by the lapels again. "I swear, Sam. Nothing on God's earth would sound silly to me. You can do anything. *Anything*. You want to chop the head off the Statue of Liberty? Put a goat on top of the Washington Monument? Tear a page out of the Gutenberg Bible? Shuffle the catalog cards in the Library of Congress? Come on, what is it?"

"You won't laugh at me?" Sam asked anxiously.

"I'll never laugh again as long as I live," Chuck sobbed.

"Well, I'd like to convince my wife that money isn't important."

"Sam!" Ruth cried. "Get them to draw up a contract. I'll admit it right now. And let me handle the business end of this."

"Now, Ruth," Sam said. "You obviously don't mean it. You'll sell the word for a million dollars, or however much you can get. That *shows* you think money is important."

Chuck was chewing on the shredded edge of his handkerchief again. "I don't know," he sighed. "Maybe we can do something there. A psychologist, maybe. Or pamphlets on heart disease. Ruth, would you read the pamphlets?"

"You're a wise one," she answered. "Hell, no, I wouldn't read the pamphlets. I've got a much better idea. Why don't you convince Sam that money *is* important?"

"We'll work on that angle, too," Chuck said. "And the misprint. We ought to be able to work that out."

"What were the directions to the recipe?" Ruth asked.

"The words," Chuck answered, "are engraved on my heart in acid. 'Pick a handful of moly in the early morning. Boil well in fresh mare's milk. Pour in a healthy amount of pale wine. Drink.' That's all."

"Well, let's see," Ruth said concentrating. "If I find the misprint, will you buy it from me?"

"Yes, yes," Chuck said feverishly. "We'll be working on that, too. Although I don't know what we could do to that recipe that we haven't tried. We've boiled it, baked it, broiled it, burned it, sun-dried it. We've tried it raw, slightly cooked, cooked solid. We've tried every possible amount of each ingredient."

"The amounts and methods of preparation don't matter that much," Sam said maddeningly. "I wouldn't go to all that trouble."

Ruth and Chuck were muttering to themselves.

"Pick a *canful*?"

"*Soil* well in fresh mare's milk?"

"Pick a handful in the *barley* morning?"

"Pour in a healthy amount of *stale* wine?"

"Blink?"

"Pink?"

"Think?"

"Oh, hell," Chuck said, "none of that makes sense. We'll have experts working on this."

"Don't go sending any experts to work on *me*," Ruth said. "Why don't you just give us some money and when Sam sees what I can do with it, maybe he'll change his mind."

"We'll see," Chuck said. "I'm going to throw this one to a battery of idea men." He dove out the door and went careening down the steps.

Sam spent the rest of the evening with his microfilm viewer while Ruth sat around muttering to herself.

"*Store* in a healthy amount of pale wine? Maybe it needs to age. *Male* wine? Sam, did they have a different wine for men and women?"

"What?"

"I said . . . Oh, never mind. *Coil* well in fresh mare's milk? Maybe you just need to twist out a little of the juice. Like bruising mint gently for a julep. Oh, I won't sleep until all this is cleared up."

Her words were truer than she thought.

The next evening Sam was visited by an apparition from a calendar. She was the sort of woman about whom wives say, "Dear, that isn't even artistic. No woman is actually *built* like that." But this one was.

The girl ran a slim, white hand through her luxuriant blond hair and smiled. "Mind if I take off my wrap?"

"Of course I mind," Ruth answered, eyeing the back-less and almost frontless black velvet gown beneath. "But go ahead. I suppose Full Head sent you to show what money can buy."

"By no means," the girl said. She immediately pulled up a chair beside Sam and ignored Ruth completely. "Sam," she said, "my name is Debbie. Full Head *did* send me. But not for the reason your wife thinks." She gave Ruth a nasty look.

Sam looked at her and frowned. "Aren't you afraid you'll catch cold, Debbie?"

"Oh, no." Debbie sprang a soft, contralto laugh that shimmied around the living room and made Ruth fear for her unborn child. "I'm so young, Sam. And warm. But how *darling* of you to be concerned."

"Well, why *did* you come?" Ruth asked in a menacing tone.

"To *learn*," the girl breathed. She breathed it on Sam's neck. "Full Head has naturally developed an interest in epigraphy. Now, our people can't hope to break the Scythian alphabet in a few days when it took Sam fifteen years. But we're thinking of setting up a special department of research in epigraphy, in honor of Sam. And I'm here," she went on, gazing up at Sam with eyes that would have been bovine had they not been blue, "to sit at the feet of the master."

"Oh, I'm not that good," Sam said modestly. "But if

you're really interested in epigraphy, I'd be glad to teach you a few basic rules."

"Interested?" the girl cried. "I'm *fascinated.* I *begged* to be sent on this assignment. I think epigraphy is the most fascinating subject in the world."

"Like hell you do," Ruth said viciously. "You can stop right now."

"You'll have to excuse my wife," Sam said apologetically. "Epigraphy always makes her nervous. I don't know what it is that annoys her so about it."

"I know," Debbie said sympathetically. "It so often happens with men of powerful intellect. Your wife simply doesn't *understand* you."

Sam looked pensively at his wife. "Ruth, is that it? You don't understand me?"

"Oh, you idiot," Ruth said. "That female's here to worm the misprint out of you. She's no more interested in epigraphy than Chuck was. *Look* at her. Never mind," Ruth said on second thought. *"Don't* look at her. Just tell her to go home."

"Did you really come to worm that word out of me?" Sam asked.

"Definitely not. Cross my heart," Debbie answered, crossing a well-developed area. "You can send me right home if I say one *word* about that misprint."

"Fair enough," Sam said with a pleased look at his wife. "All right, now. Let's get started."

"Let's!" Debbie moved in closer to him.

"Epigraphy, as you probably know, is from the Greek 'epi' and 'graphe' meaning—"

"Oh, *Sam,"* Ruth cried. "I can't stand this."

"Well, you go on to bed, dear. I know you're not interested."

"Yes," Debbie said with a sweet smile. "You go to bed. We can carry on."

"I'll bet you can," Ruth said, and slammed the door behind her.

The next morning was Sunday. Ruth arose late and red-eyed. She fixed one cup of coffee, one egg and one piece of toast. When Sam came into the kitchen sniffing the air hungrily, Ruth turned on the radio with a vicious twist and continued eating to a deafening account of the morning news.

Sam got himself a bowl of what he usually referred to as flaked cardboard, turned down the radio and ate unhappily.

Suddenly Ruth forgot how mad she was and put her hand on Sam's. "Listen!" she cried. The familiar nasal voice of the newscaster was excited.

"What's behind the lanolin curtain? What happens to the hair that Full Head grows? Why is there an armed guard around the Full Head Building? Don't call your senator yet. We expect to have a full report on the seven o'clock news tonight. . . . *Flash!* There has just been an attempted lynch of a Manhattan barber by three baldheaded men in gray flannel suits."

"Well," Ruth said vindictively, "I guess *that* ought to teach Chuck Bradford crime does not pay."

The doorbell rang.

"I think we'd have more privacy around here," Sam said gently but reprovingly, "if you didn't keep speaking of the devil."

Chuck slunk in the door with paranoidal glances over his left shoulder. "They're after me," he said, sinking onto the shabby sofa.

"Good for them!" Ruth commented. "I'll buy the rope."

"*Kick* a handful of moly?" Chuck asked Sam, not very hopefully.

"If you like," Sam answered, "but it won't help your formula."

At this point of impasse in the history of hirsute western civilization, Fate again took a hand. A rather hairy but very capable hand, extending from a black flannel sleeve, pushed the doorbell still warm from Chuck Bradford's caress.

"The President of the United States," said the respectable but anonymous-looking man attached to the capable hand, "would like to see you."

"I had a previous engagement," Sam said with an uncertain frown. "Of course—"

"The President, too, has a full schedule."

"Oh, of course." Sam went peacefully.

"Creeping Socialism!" Chuck shouted after they left. "Government intervention! If they make that hair restorer a government project—hell, what can you expect after twenty years of the Re-Deal?"

"Now who could Sam have had an engagement with?" Ruth mused.

The doorbell rang. This time Fate had a soft white hand.

"Oh, he's not here!" Debbie exclaimed, fluttering in disappointment. "He was supposed to show me through a collection of ancient coins."

"Goodbye," Ruth said clammily, and shut the door behind Debbie after a good, hard shove. She turned to Chuck. "O.K. I was going to wait and watch you get lynched. But I want to get that woman off Sam's neck. You draw up a contract and I'll give you the correct formula for Sam's hair restorer."

"You mean all this time you've known it?"

"Not all this time. But I had a lot of time to myself last night. And it occurred to me that Sam must have a carbon copy of his manuscript, and I looked and there it was."

"You go find some neighbors to witness," Chuck said, "and I'll do the writing."

Sam was gone most of the day. He opened the door to find Debbie on the sofa and Ruth in the armchair, studiously ignoring each other.

"The President of the United States," he announced, "will not go bald."

"She won't go away," Ruth said.

"Why should I?" Debbie asked, smiling just for Sam.

"Because Full Head already *has* the formula," Ruth volunteered. "You're no longer needed."

"Do *you* want me to go, Sam?"

"Now she wants your money," Ruth said.

"What money? What is this? And where's dinner?"

"I found the carbon copy of your manuscript and sold it to Chuck. And now I didn't get rid of her after all." Ruth could no longer control herself. "You don't *love* me any more," she sobbed.

"Yes I do, dear."

"Well, you won't long. Tell her to go away."

"We mustn't be impolite. What makes her think I have money?"

"I just told you. I sold your word to Full Head."

"Just so Debbie wouldn't come around? Not for money?"

"I had to sell it for *something*. But yes, I mostly wanted to get rid of Debbie."

"Dear, that was very misguided of you, but underneath I think your motive was not monetary. Suppose I told you we weren't going to make any money after all."

"That would be *wonderful*," Ruth said. "That would solve all our problems."

"What do you mean?" Debbie asked. Her ingenuous air began to thicken a little.

"I gave the correct translation of the Scythian formula to the American Government. You couldn't sell it, anyway, Ruth. It's common property. No copyrights back in 450 B.C., you know. All I did was translate it."

"But Ruth's got a contract!" Debbie cried.

"Won't hold water, or whatever contracts hold. But don't worry about your company, Debbie. I took care of Full Head. Chuck Bradford's worked so hard over this. The United States Government is going to farm out production to Full Head. They just want to control cheap distribution overseas. As the President says, a head full of hair is a heart full of good will."

"No money?" Debbie asked.

"No money."

"No Debbie," said Debbie, and she was gone, like Snow upon the Desert's dusty Face.

"Do I get any dinner?" Sam asked.

"Yes. But why '*Lick* a handful of moly'?"

"Some enzyme in human spit, I'm sure. But you boil it later so it's perfectly sanitary. What do we have for—"

"Meatloaf again," Ruth said happily. "I *like* meatloaf. You're right. Money isn't important. And Sam, I'm sorry that I sold the word, I hate to go above you." Here the brown eyes lower fell. "Because, you see, I love you."